Tommy Smurlee
and
Dunster's Camp of
Mystery & Inventions

Judith Rolfs

Copyright @ Judith Rolfs 2016

WHAT READERS AND THEIR PARENTS
ARE SAYING ABOUT THE ADVENTURES OF TOMMY
SMURLEE:

"Abby (age 10) just loved the Tommy Smurlee books and has read both. It's great to have her read books that are contemporary, entertaining, and teach good values."

John F., Orlando, FL

"My son (Nathan, age 8) really loved them. He adored the character of Tommy. In fact just the other day he pulled them out again and he was so excited to see how you had signed them. He asked if I thought there would every be another one in the series and I said I don't know. If you ever write another one, please let me know. Also know that you touched my son's life in a very positive way with your books."

Amy B., Racine, WI

"I really love the book Adventures of Tommy Smurlee. I hope you write more."

Ranger age 13

"It's a great, fast-moving, fun book. Some day I want to write a book like this"

Drew, age13

"I read it two times in one weekend and at least 10 more times since."

Steven, age 11

"My mom read The Adventures of Tommy Smurlee aloud to me. I loved it!"

Dan, age 7

Dedication

For Drew,
Jack,
Katie
Steven,
Daniel,
Kyle,
Joshua
and Anna
because they know the wonders of
creativity and imagination
and
Tamara, Pam, David, & Dan,
the first to travel the path.

Table of Contents

Chapter 1
Dunster's Camp

"Dunster's Camp of Mystery and Inventions. One mile. Come and be amazed!" Grandpa Smurlee read the road sign aloud as they drove by. He turned and smiled at his grandson. "Almost there."

Twelve-year-old Tommy shot upright in the back seat and grabbed the camp brochure from his Red Notebook. Words jumped off the page as he read them aloud again. "For the Camper Looking for Something More! Master the Hedge Maze —Thousands of Mysterious Shrubs, Expand Your Imagination in Imagino Lab with Skyscape and Motion-o-rama, Invent in our Twickle Lab, and play Slap/Dash – Dunster's Challenging Team Sport! For goose-chilling excitement there's Monster Mania and History of Mystery!"

"Read about the other activities too, Tommy," Grandma urged from her front seat next to Grandpa.

Tommy ran through the brochure titles. "Unravel Dunster's Great Unsolved Mystery of the Summer With Your Teammates." "Explore the Secret Springs and Hidden Halls." "Fully Equipped With the Latest in Dream Machines and Dunster's Inventions." "Dream It! Do It! D-I-D-I is Dunster's Motto!"

"Gives me shivers," Grandma said. "Wish I could go. What else?"

"You remember the rest, Grandma," Tommy said. "Now taking camper applications for our summer program. Pre-register by appointment. Limited openings."

Grandma Smurlee grinned over her shoulder at Tommy. Then her eyes became shiny. "We'll miss you terribly, but this camp sounds like so much fun for you."

I hope I like it, Tommy thought, clutching his Red Notebook.

He thought back to last Thursday when he first heard about Dunster's. Grandpa had been looking for his rocker, which Tommy had been using for motion experiments in the garage. Grandpa dragged the rocker into the family room where Tommy and Grandma Smurlee were making chocolate chip dough creatures using designs Tommy had made on the computer.

"Sorry, Grandpa, I forgot to bring it back in," Tommy said.

"No problem." Grandpa had sat down to read his favorite magazine, The Natural Adventurer. Deep down Grandpa Smurlee had the blood of an adventurer in him but only read about excursions.

Suddenly Grandpa yelled, "Listen to this!" He read Dunster's Camp ad aloud. It says it's "Ideal for children with strong curiosity and a sense of adventure. Know anybody like that?"

Tommy did a handstand and squealed. "Can I go, please, please?"

"I don't know. I wonder if you'd be lonely." Grandpa said. "Six weeks is a long time."

"I think I could handle it."

Grandma had coaxed Grandpa. "I'm always wanting Tommy to play with other kids more."

"I hope I'll get along with them." Tommy munched a cookie "I'm different, you know, with my inventing and always studying how things work."

"That's why this camp may be perfect," Grandma said.

The next night he and Grandma contacted Tommy's parents, wildlife researchers and missionaries in Africa who traveled for long stretches into dangerous territory where children weren't safe.

Tommy added a P.S. to Grandpa's e-mail "Being with Grandma and Grandpa Smurlee is next best to being with you, Mom and Dad. But I think Dunster's Camp would be cool."

Tommy's parents e-mailed back the next day. "The camp sounds great. Visit by all means. Then, if Grandma and Grandpa approve, go."

And so here they were. Tommy's hands felt sweaty. He swallowed deeply. He'd never been away from family for more than a week before. He put the brochure back in the flap of his Red Notebook.

Grandma seemed to sense his concern. "No time to be sad at a camp of Mystery and Inventions. We'll be the ones missing you." She felt a slight chill and reached over to turn down the car's air conditioning.

Grandpa Smurlee tilted his head toward the back seat. "Tommy, I wonder how many afternoons you and I have spent exploring."

Tommy checked his Red Notebook. "This past year 68."

Tommy collected maps. He printed them on his computer and used them to direct Grandpa. He brought his Red Notebook everywhere. He liked measuring, counting and recording everything —the length of spider's legs, the number of branches swaying in the wind, the time between the toots of a train.

Grandma laughed. "You had me down every road within a hundred miles!"

"Sure did. Plenty of stops for observations, too, the gravel quarry, old barns, train depot, you name it," Grandpa reminisced.

"I remember when Tommy was three." Grandma slapped her hand against her knee. "Your mother worried about your focus on numbers and asked Doctor Dikkle about it. The family doctor said, "Tommy has the Analyzing and Counting Disorder. He'll probably outgrow it."

"Never has yet!" Grandpa snorted. "Nine years later he's still recording measurements and thoughts in his Red Notebook."

Tommy snapped the book shut. "I hope to use them some day for some purpose, but can't imagine what." Tommy gulped. He rode the last mile to Dunster's Camp getting more nervous and more curious by the minute.

Chapter 2
The Mysterious Entrance

Tommy gasped when the Honda rounded the last curve.

"This can't be a camp. It's too big!" Grandma whispered almost breathless.

A long driveway ahead led to an ancient stone building, five stories tall in the center with two-story wings shooting off three sides. Several smaller wooden buildings in the distance looked like boathouses and activity centers. All the structures sat on a huge slab of land backed by water and bordered by forest.

"This can't be a camp!" Grandma repeated.

A gigantic playing field on the right was divided into hundreds of squares about three foot by three outlined in white. A thick forest extended along the left side of the as far as they could see. The land in front of the main building, where the driveway ended, was open and grassy.

Fog, heavy as a king's cloak, unfolded from the lake giving a misty coating to all the buildings at Dunster's.

"How strange!" Grandpa Smurlee said. "We saw no fog at all until now."

Grandma relaxed against the car seat. "Well, this definitely looks interesting, Tommy. You'll have lots of room to explore."

"Right!" Tommy eyes darted back and forth from the camp to his notebook. His fingers raced across the sketch he was making of Dunster's layout. "It's impressive, Grandpa, don't you think?"

Grandpa answered with a long whistle. "Let's head down the driveway and get a closer look."

"Wait. Look at the pillars!" Tommy stuck his head out the car window.

Two greenstone pillars about six feet high stood halfway down the drive leading to the buildings. Purple balls shot out of each pillar, five feet into the air and then fell back into the pillar. The balls were the size used for tennis, but looked much harder. Plop, plop, three balls at a time popped out in a perfect arc.

They stopped at the pillars to watch as the balls popped back into the column in perfect order. Every few seconds they shot out again.

As they sizzled into the air they gave off a steamy scent of vanilla.

"Hmmn, smells like sugar cookies," Grandpa said. "I like this place already."

How do they do that? Tommy wondered. He reached into his duffel bag, pulled out his special magnifying glasses and slipped the band over his head.

Minutes later Tommy was atop the car holding his Red Notebook and peering at one of the pillars.

"I think it's completely hollow inside," he called down.

"Be careful, be careful," Grandma repeated.

Tommy dabbed his finger at one ball and touched it lightly as it popped past, but didn't try to stop it. The ball was hot. When touched the fragrance of cookies baking changed to skunk smell.

Grandpa yelled, "Let's go." He restarted the car and rolled up the windows.

"Incredible!" Tommy jumped quickly back into the car.

"Yuk, it stinks," Grandma said.

Tommy made a note in his book. "One more minute, Grandpa." He pulled his stopwatch from his pocket. "I need to time them. Ten seconds out, balance in the air for seven seconds, down in five." They sat in the car with motor whirring for several minutes.

"The rhythm stays the same. Okay, Grandpa, thanks. You can drive on."

Grandma glanced in the backseat at Tommy sketching a picture of the balls in his Red Notebook. He finished and took off the special headband he'd assembled with two lens that enlarged everything to super size. He liked examining details with his magnifiers.

What could he check next? Tommy's brain whizzed. Sometimes he could almost hear it working. A horrible thought came to him. What if he was bored and didn't like Dunster's Camp?

It almost seemed like Grandma read his mind. "This will be your delightful home away from home for several weeks, Tommy." He noted Grandma used her super positive voice —the one she used when she wanted to convince herself of something also, probably to hide her sadness. She wouldn't see him every day if he went here.

"Grandma and Grandpa, before we go in, I've been thinking," Tommy mumbled. "If I go to this camp, I can't be coming home every weekend. It's three hours away. I hope you won't be too bored without me." Tommy thought boredom was one of the worst possible things that could happen to anyone.

Grandma Smurlee thrust out her lower lip. "As long as you have a good time here we'll manage."

Tommy loved Grandma very much. He knew she always wanted the very best for him. Grandpa, too.

Grandpa parked the car. Together they walked hesitantly to the center building with its sprawling wings.

Tommy was glad Grandma wore her walking shoes. He was very protective of her. The three of them hiked up twenty-four steps following an arrow sign that said "Entrance."

They found themselves on a massive concrete porch that ran across the front of the building. Dotted here and there across the porch were doors of different sizes and shapes in an irregular row. Tommy counted them – fourteen doors.

Grandpa shook his head. "Where do we go in?"

Grandma Smurlee scrunched her shoulders to her neck. She always did that when she was thinking hard. "How would we know? There's no entrance sign on any door."

"Let's try them all," Grandpa said.

"Wait. We can figure this out," Tommy said. "It's a bit of a challenge." His eyes gleamed as he studied the first door. It was very short. They'd have to stoop to enter it. The second, a massive arched oak door, the kind used in churches, was by far the biggest.

"Too obvious, that one," Tommy said. The next door was smooth wood, painted black. Tommy walked past. "Not dark to start," he muttered.

The fourth door was gold. "Too fancy," Tommy said.

A green glow and a musty smell came from under the fifth door. Tommy sniffed and pointed. "How about this one? It smells old, ancient."

Grandpa looked at Grandma. "Let's try it."

They followed Tommy into a maze of darkened shadows. Every few feet the corridor took a sharp turn and they bumped against a damp wall of cold metal. The green glow gave just enough light to see before it began to fade.

Tommy felt ahead with his arms. Cold concrete top to bottom. Suddenly the glow went out entirely.

"Drat! We've reached a dead end. We'll need to try another door," Tommy directed.

They groped their way back hoping they were returning the same way they'd come.

Grandma, who was behind Tommy, suddenly let out an ear-piercing scream and flung her arms against her head. "Something flapped around my hair."

Grandpa couldn't stop fast enough and stumbled into her.

"Ouch! You stepped on my foot!" Grandma screeched.

"Well, don't just stop!"

"Probably a bat," Tommy said.

"Whatever, it's somewhere ahead of us and I'm not moving," Grandma said.

"Yes, you are." Grandpa put his arm around her waist and led her gently along. "You can't stay here."

Grandma grit her teeth and went forward.

Eventually the three ended up outside. The air had gotten chillier.

"Let's ask someone for help," Grandma suggested.

"Who?" Grandpa looked through the mist but could see no one. "Not even another car." Their Honda sat alone in the huge parking lot.

"It looks like everything is closed," Grandma said, "but how can that be? We have an appointment."

"Maybe we got the date wrong," Grandpa said.

"No, I'm sure it's today. You'd think with a camp this size, there'd be somebody working on the grounds at least." Grandma sat down on the steps. "You find the office and come get me."

Grandpa looked around, a little nervously then helped Grandma up. "Come on. We're not leaving you alone."

Tommy studied the doors again. Two neon arrows lit up and pointed to the door painted red. "How about that door."

Tommy walked over and opened it. His grandparents followed him in. After going down a long winding corridor they found themselves outside again.

"Double Drat, we've got to figure this out," Grandpa said.

Tommy studied the doors again. He opened the sixth door and signaled Grandma and Grandpa to follow.

Three pigeons flew past them eager to get out. "This is the way," Tommy said more confidently than he felt.

Soon they found themselves in another hall. At the end was a large double door with a sign on it. When they got closer Grandpa Smurlee read aloud, "Head Camp Director, Mr. Croggle."

"At last," Grandma said. She knocked firmly on the door.

A voice that sounded like a cross between a frog's croak and a wolf's yowl said, "Come in."

Tommy held his breath.

Only candles lighted the large room they entered. It had a musty smell —the same as the hall they'd been in —like an old wooden dresser. A hefty man with a bald circle on the top of his head was seated backwards in a chair behind a long metal table. He appeared to be looking out a window behind him only it wasn't a real window, but a glass painted with a forest scene.

"You must be the Smurlees! Nice work. You found me! It took only eleven minutes. Excellent!"

"What the samhill was that door confusion for?" Grandpa asked.

"Ah, just a little preliminary sleuth work, basic of course, but it sets the tone well for a Camp of Mystery and Inventions, don't you think? I'm Director Croggle. Please be seated."

The Director's voice was cheery, but when he swiveled in his chair his owl-shaped face scowled angrily at them. He noticed them staring at his face. "Please disregard this look. I got stuck in a dream experiment yesterday —a bad one. I can't get rid of it until tomorrow's activity session in Dreamology. The staff checks out all activities before the campers participate to be sure they're safe. Try not to let my appearance distract you."

"My goodness!" Grandma didn't know what else to say.

Tommy said, "No problem, sir."

"Please, please, take a seat. The Director pointed at four metal chairs across from the table. Grandpa dutifully sat down in the farthest one. As soon as he was seated a buzzer sounded, the floorboards separated and he disappeared through the floor.

Grandma gasped and grabbed Tommy's shoulder to keep him from disappearing.

Faster than an eye blink, Grandpa emerged from an opening in the floor across the room, still sitting on his chair.

Director Croggle slapped his knee. "I so enjoy having first time visitors!"

"If you don't mind we'll stand," Tommy said.

Grandpa was beaming. "Can I do that again? It was great."

"Perhaps later, Sir, if time allows. Now down to business. What questions do you have about Dunster's?"

Tommy was never shy around adults, only with kids his own age, so he spoke right up. "We'd like to look around the camp, sir."

"Yes, of course, but paperwork before pleasure. Fill out this application form, then I'll give you a personal tour."

Grandpa Smurlee said, "But we're not sure yet if my grandson will be attending."

"Of course he'll want to, but here use this pen with the disappearing ink for now." Director Croggle whipped a lemon yellow pen from his vest pocket. "If after the tour, you decide Tommy's not coming blow on the ink and it will disappear. You may hang on to the application until you leave if it makes you feel better."

Grandma busied herself with the form after examining and sniffing the pen.

Grandpa Smurlee pulled out the list of questions he had written. "Excuse me, Director Croggle, but a Camp of Mystery and Inventions, is a bit, er, unusual. What do Dunster's campers, er, do, when they're here?"

"Do? Sir, there are a thousand and two possibilities listed in our camper manual that he'll get when he checks in." Director Croggle harrumphed.

Tommy immediately jotted the number in his notebook.

"A camp experience here is the finest known in this century. It prepares children to be adults who can think, imagine and create —the greatest of skills!"

The Director took a sip from some thick clear liquid in a glass on the table. "May I offer you some sweet water, a bit thicker and tastier than you're used to probably, but packed with nutrients, created by a former camper in fact."

They declined.

"Now where was I? Oh yes," Director Croggle said. "Who worked on the original main frame computer? Who was involved in the first manned moon exploration? Past Dunster campers, that's who! I assure you every camper except a Downer loves the Camp of Mystery and Inventions and hates it when the eight-week session is over and they must leave for home. Campers come back year after year until they turn seventeen. That's our age limit."

Grandma Smurlee noticed Tommy sitting on the edge of his chair with his pencil flying across the pages of his Red Notebook. She sighed, "Sorry to interrupt, sweetie, I need to write on this application form your favorite fruit and your favorite pet. Shall I say apple or tomato? And is your favorite pet Kia, your boa constrictor or Ellie, your eel?"

"Apple in winter, tomato in summer, and Kia, definitely Kia, Grandma." Tommy returned to listening to the Director's words.

"Our campers play hard, but they love the challenges except, as I said, for the Downers of course."

"Who are they?" Tommy asked.

"Every camp, every school has some. Downers are complainers who never like anything. They get stuck in so many "what-ifs" and "why-didn'ts" that they can't let their imaginations free. They usually don't last long here. We try to weed them out their first week, but some are stubborn about hanging on." Director Croggle put on his pair of green wire spectacles to stare closely at Tommy possibly to determine if he'd be a Downer.

Grandma Smurlee was quietly looking at the pictures on the wall. Tommy saw her squinting hard to make out the scenes.

Director Croggle noticed, too. "They're all quite hazy," he said, "Thought Pictures, Mrs. Smurlee, you can make them what you like. Ahh, that's the beauty of personal art!"

"Interesting," she said looking at him as if he were out of his mind. "Well, if Tommy comes here, I want you to know Tommy is a light sleeper. His bed at our home is a canoe fitted with a mattress that he made with his Grandpa. It rotates back and forth as he sleeps." She stopped to beam at her husband who was busily examining the floorboards at the moment. "Anyway," Grandma Smurlee continued, "Tommy usually wakes between 4 A. M and 5 A.M. and works on his computer until 6 A.M. I hope that's okay. And by the way may he bring it?"

"The computer or the bed?"

Grandma giggled, "Not the bed, of course."

"The camp provides each camper with a computer to use while here. Some of our activities require it. In fact each morning Tommy will need a new printout of his activities because they change daily. Now madam. Is there anything else we should need to know – dietary concerns, health issues?"

"Tommy's in good health, but I do have one last question," Grandma said.

Yes?" Director Croggle drummed his pen on his note pad.

"I want to be certain that Tommy will be safe here. Are the campers supervised around the clock?"

"Our campers may roam freely on Dunster's property, but the perimeter of our grounds has an excellent security system, seldom cracked. Here's a list of testimonials from parents and past campers. You'll read how highly Dunster's Camp is praised. Read it at your leisure." He spoke cheerily, but was still frowning deeply.

Grandma grabbed the paper and said, "Thank you."

Grandpa added, "Of course we'll call some of these parents to verify their approval."

"Naturally." Director Croggle stood up. "Now I'll take you into our Dream Wing and show you the Dreamology and Imagino labs although they're empty. We don't officially start sessions until mid-June."

"I have a question, Director Croggle," Tommy said while walking alongside him. "How do those balls at the entrance stay in motion and make such a perfect arc when there's no strings or motors, not even a fan."

Croggle chuckled. "Lesson Number 1. Not every mystery is meant to be solved. The beauty of the pure mystery is, it will go on forever."

No, Tommy thought, *I want to solve them all!*

After the visit to Dunster's Tommy stayed up all night thoughtfully going over the numbers: 108 acres of campground, forty-three acres were woods. Campers were assigned two to a room, forty-nine campers in all. Average camp room size twelve by eighteen. Best of all, invention potential was incredible, mystery opportunities limitless. *Why I could approach numbers close to infinity there!*

Chapter 3
Keeper of the Supplies

Tommy arrived at Dunster's Camp of Mystery and Inventions two weeks later with one large suitcase for his clothes, his Red Notebook and his tennis racket. When he waved goodbye to his grandparents at the circle drive he felt a drop of salt water on his face and a stab of sadness in his heart. Grandma waved a handkerchief from the car window and dabbed at her nose with another.

Tommy watched until their car was out of sight.

He walked back to the front door of camp feeling a shivery thrill as he entered the massive oak front door on the far right, which was now open during daylight hours.

He gave himself a talk in his head, *Make the best of it, Tommy, you're off on an adventure.* It's what his dad would say, he knew.

Where to now, he wondered? He'd already been to the Director's office. Croggle had shown him the tunnel route to the wings and had given him a secret voice command to use on the inner concrete doors to the various halls. Tommy carried a card in his pocket with the name of his roommate and his room number.

"You're on your own, except for the Sunmaker, of course." The Director had said. "Go get your books and supplies from Counselor Filey so you'll have what you need.

Camp activities start officially tomorrow. Here's the list. No need to look at it, just give it to the Keeper of the Supplies on the top floor. Take the Wind Whoosher up. You'll catch it on the second floor." With that Croggle shooed Tommy off.

Whoosher? Whatever that is, Tommy thought. *And where were the other campers? Shouldn't some be arriving by now?*

Tommy took the stairs from the first to the second floor. Then he started looking for signs of a Wind Whoosher. He had no idea what he was looking for, but Croggle seemed to think he should know so Tommy decided to try to figure it out.

In the middle of the central hall Tommy came upon a steel door that looked like the entrance to an elevator. Alongside it was a red lever that pulled sideways. A buzzer sounded and the door slid open with a thud.

When Tommy peered into the darkness a light flashed on. There was no elevator inside. Just a thick honey-colored rope, some kind of pulley. While he watched the rope started to move. A small boy zoomed past him hanging on the rope.

Suddenly the boy came back. Had he seen Tommy waiting?

"Need a whoosh?"

"I sure do, but I'm not sure how."

"Oh, it's quite easy, once you know. Find the ball on the wall rack with the number of the floor you want and put it in the slot for that floor. The wind is channeled into a machine that lets out a big whoosh, one per second. If you're hanging on, and hang on tight mind you, it will take you as far as you want to go."

"I need to go the top floor."

"That's the fifth. You'll need fifteen whooshes, three take you up one floor. It's a bit of a math challenge. Keeps the Drubbins from messing with something that could be dangerous."

"Looks like you do it easily."

The boy smiled and held out his hand. "My name's Mr. Toodle. I'm eleven, a bit on the short side for my age, I know, first thing you see when you look at me. But I'm in the Big Brain Bunch so I can carry my own. Don't mess with me. Just a friendly warning, of course."

"I never would, Mr. Toodle. Are you old enough to be called a Mr.?"

"Of course not, I like the sound of it though. Toodle will do for you. Now grab a hold. I'll ride with you the first time to make sure you know how to handle yourself."

"Thanks."

"Find the ball that says your floor and pop it in the slot. The ball reader machine will feed the wind program in for you —exactly the amount of wind whoosh needed to propel you to your floor. Ready, here we go."

Whoosh! To the top they went.

"Faster than most elevators," Toodle bragged, "but not all. We're working on more speed."

Tommy jumped off at the top floor.

"See you." Toodle had already grabbed ball number two, tossed it in the slot and disappeared as the door closed behind him.

Tommy looked around the dark attic with its wood plank floors. Around him were several rooms divided by cedar walls. The hall smelled like cedar - the inside of the drawers in the old dresser Grandma Smurlee had in the guest room.

In the dim light he made out signs outside the rooms. One said "Keeper of the Supplies." Then he saw that every room had a sign with the same words "Keeper of the Supplies." Oh well. He opened the door and peered into the closest room. "Anybody here?"

No one answered. Tommy saw books, games, racquets and balls everywhere. Some of the balls were flat like a tightly stuffed beanbag and the word "Popple" was written on them. Every which way Tommy walked he dodged equipment. Books were piled in stacks on tables, too, all the way up to the covered skylight in the roof. Why *have a skylight if it's covered?* Tommy wondered.

When Tommy reached the third room, also full of supplies, an old man with an elf-like face topped by a tall pointy hat slipped off a cot and shuffled over on floppy suede slippers. He wore a faded brown suit and a crumpled yellow shirt and carried a short stick.

"Excuse me, sir, I'm looking for the Keeper of the Supplies."

"I am he, and I suppose you want something of me!"

"You work here? But I saw your bed."

The Keeper took off his pointed brown hat and scratched his head. He was bald except for one tuft of white hair at the center of his head. "And why not? I never leave this place. I eat and sleep here. I'm the Keeper of the Supplies. I do most of my sorting at night, and sleep a bit during the day." He peered closely at Tommy coming within inches of his face. "Ah, you must be a new camper."

"Yes, sir. I'm Tommy Smurlee here for my supplies."

"Most sad."

Why did he say that? Tommy felt cold all over and confused.

"And you're a wondering why we're up to the roof almost?"

Tommy stammered, "No sir, I wasn't."

"Save it, save it. I'm not going to answer except to say we used to keep the supplies in the cellar. Too damp for the books. Then we came to the attic, too light at first. Now we keep black cloths on the windows and skylights and drape black sheets over the supply tables each night. These mystery secrets must be preserved. Some of our books are out-of-print. We've some of the few copies still in existence."

"Wow!" That was all Tommy could think to say. He had no idea what books this strange man was talking about.

"Now don't ask me anything else because I'm not going to answer you," the Keeper of the Supplies said gruffly. "I have work to do."

"Excuse me sir," Tommy said, trying to sound very polite. He didn't want the Keeper yelling at him again.

"Sir? My name is Filey, don't sir me, sir."

"Well then, Filey, I need my camp supplies."

"Most unfortunate. I always grieve when any of my supplies leave."

Tommy wanted to ask why Filey was in charge of the books and supplies then, but he didn't dare.

"Well, let's get on with it," Filey said. "How can I find them for you until I know the activities you're taking?"

"Yes, sir, sorry. This must be what you need." Tommy handed the Keeper the sealed envelope from his pocket. "Director Croggle said I'm not to see it yet. I have three Unknown activities each week. He said you'll know which."

"Of course I do, the Unknowns, the ones with the big "U" next to them! Stop giving me directions. What do you think? Was I born last month?"

Tommy looked at The Keeper of the Supplies' gnarled grape vine fingers and his stooped body. More like he'd been born about a hundred years ago. Tommy blinked and choked out the rest of his orders from Director Croggle. "The supplies for each Unknown should be put into a separate brown shopping bag and stapled shut." Tommy shut his eyes waiting for an explosion.

"I suppose you expect me to label them Unknowns 1, 2, and 3, too?" he barked.

Tommy opened his eyes. That wasn't too bad. "Yes, please. Thank you sir."

The old man grumbled again and shuffled over to the back tables. He kept shaking his head. He used his short stick to help him sort through items. One by one he pulled out books, games, and sports equipment and crossed them off the list.

Every now and then Filey made a comment like, "They're letting you do that! Shucks, be glory" or "I dunno know what's come into Croggle's brain."

Tommy looked at the book titles the Keeper was stacking on one end of his dusty desk: *Imago the Great Imaginator*, *Tips for Polishing Your Brain* authored by Beanie Fooster, *Fun with Your Mind* by Whiz Waddle.

"We've also *Gizmos and Gadgets Galore* by Gustave Makem, *Mystery Mania* by Mark Sanctum. And here's *Games You've Never Heard Of* by Q. B. Funn, You might want those for extra reading. I'll stick them in just in case."

"Ahhh! Here's a good one, *If You Dare* by Ican Dooit! It's one of my favorites. Ican inspired me to try my hand at writing, blimey if I haven't. Smurlee, see those manuscripts? Filey pointed to a table over at the side of his bed. Nine books, none published, can't seem to get one quite right yet. But I'm getting closer."

Filey hobbled over to another stack of books in cardboard boxes. "Here's a new one, *Creations of the Mind* by Hoppy Dooster. I haven't had time to unpack these."

Tommy squinted to read the titles in the darkness.

"What else is on your list?" The Keeper shone his tiny penlight on the list again and read aloud, "Slap/Dash equipment, a lance for Medieval Battle, *The Story of Dunster's* by Director Cary Croggle himself. *On Dreaming*, by Dr. Ronald Sleepless. Also books by Arthur Conan Doyle and several of the great mystery writers."

I'll never use all these supplies, Tommy thought.

"Alright, what's your name again?" The Keeper looked down at his list.

"Tommy Smurlee. Thanks for your help, Sir."

"It's part of my job, not that I like taking time from the rest of my work, not one bit."

"What else do you do up here?"

The Keeper of the Supplies pointed to an alcove just big enough for two people. "We keep one of the earliest editions of the *Great Book of Holy Words* in the room over there. Part of my job is guarding the Holy Words and seeing that not a word or thought is ever changed. And of course I spend hours searching out the greatest books for our Dunnies."

"Sounds like a fun job."

"So every job's supposed to be fun, huh? You think that!"

"No, I didn't say, I mean, interesting would be nice. Well, I better get going."

"Good. Off with you." He handed three shopping bags to Tommy and one heavy canvas bag with the lance sticking out. "Make sure you use these with respect, you hear, or there'll be no more books or supplies from me!"

"Thanks for your help."

"There was plenty of it I gave, too. We talked about this and that. I'm all talked out, don't you know. Get familiar with these items before camp starts."

Tommy placed the smaller bags into the big one and slung it over his shoulder feeling like the mythical Santa Claus getting ready to slide down a chimney. Only Santa's bag was lighter on the way down.

Out in the hall the Wind Whoosher was unoccupied. He chose number three, positioned the ball and took off.

Tommy whooshed back and forth to a few more floors just for fun before getting off at the second. He dragged his bag toward the dorm rooms.

Tommy reread his roommate's name, Piney Putilla. Tommy Smurlee. Room 685. He was in no hurry to meet his roommate, but he was getting tired dragging this heavy bag of supplies. The muscles in both his arms ached from hanging on to the pulley with one hand and the gigantic book bag with the other. He could use a rest. Maybe he'd even go to bed early. All of a sudden Tommy was feeling a little sad.

Tomorrow would be Saturday, his first day of camp. Grandma used to bake oatmeal cookies on Saturday. They'd sit at the kitchen table and talk. He tried to remember why he thought it would be a good idea to leave his grandparents for six weeks to come here. He ran his fingers through his short brown hair and shook his head —mustn't think about Grandma and Grandpa now.

Tommy double-checked his map of the camp layout. One more last long hall and he'd be at the dorm wing. The room numbers were in Roman numerals. It took him awhile to translate the number —Room 685.

Should he knock? Was his bunkmate inside? He rapped lightly. No answer. He touched the door handle like it was coated with poison skin pellets. Unlocked. He pushed the door inward a couple of inches, peeked into the room, then shut the door as fast as he could.

Tommy scratched his head. How could this possibly be a camp dorm room? It was way too nice. A living room with a round couch revolved slowly in a circle. He'd glimpsed a refrigerator on a green wagon.

Tommy checked the number again—685. This had to be right. He opened the door all the way. Sure enough! One of the two closet doors had his name printed on a laminated plastic tag. Tommy gazed around cautiously, then pulled his bag of supplies inside.

Opposite the revolving sofa were two beds and two dressers arranged in a large alcove.

Someone's clothes were already on the one bed, neatly folded in stacks. Piney must have arrived before him.

Tommy noticed two cages next to two dressers and two beds. One cage had a huge lizard in it. The other was empty. Tommy looked away. If only he could have brought Kia, but new campers weren't allowed to have pets their first session. Tommy wished he were clinging to his snake's skin right now. He longed to stroke Kia.

Instead he opened his duffel bag and began sticking his clothes into the closet beside his bed. Not having a brother or sister, he'd never had to share a room with anyone before. He was more than a little worried.

Tommy jumped when the door opened with a bang.

He took one look at his roommate and swallowed deeply. He was expecting a kid, not a giant. Piney must be five-foot-ten. His head was topped by a bush of dark brown hair in tight curls. He looked like a tree walking. Piney was supposed to be fourteen according to Croggle who said Dunster's always assigned experienced campers to first-timers.

Piney brushed past Tommy with eyes straight ahead tossing out a quick "Hi." He slung his bag of supplies off his shoulder. It thudded on the floor. "That Filey better get some manners!"

Two other guys, younger and smaller, bounded in behind Piney. The younger boy spoke first . "Hi, I'm Blake and this is my brother Quid. We're the Hammond stepbrothers."

Quid had skin tanned the color of brown gravy and hair dark as night. Blake had green eyes and reddish-brown hair.

Quid added, "He's eleven, I'm twelve-years old."

Blake, then Quid, shook hands with Tommy. "Hey Piney, where's your manners," Blake asked.

Piney waved a claw-like hand in Tommy's direction. Then he moved his stacks of clothes to his dresser drawers. When he finished he stretched out on his bed with headphones in place.

Great, Piney's a neatnik, Tommy thought unhappily. Tommy had two different modes, super order or total mess. It all depended on how deep he was into an experiment or a mystery. Oh well, they'd work it out.

"We're in the room next door," Quid Hammond said.

"Super!" Tommy tried not to stare at Blake's unusual clothing. He'd seen baggy clothes before, but never any that bulged with pockets on front and back and even on the sleeves. Some pockets were long and thin, some small and square, a few ran the length of Blake's arm or leg. Every pocket was stuffed with something. Tommy saw the end of a screwdriver sticking out, a comic book, packets of hot chocolate. *What all could possibly be in there,* he wondered.

Quid said, "If you ever need something, you can probably find it in one of Blake's sixty-plus pockets."

"Smur, you're going Dunster's," Blake said. "This is our second year, Piney's fourth."

Tommy nodded. "I hope so. By the way, if you don't mind I'd prefer being called Tommy to Smur. No big deal though."

"Sure, Smur. " Blake laughed. "Just joking, Tommy."

Tommy had never seen such skinny guys. The brothers' shoulders and arms hung like wire coat hangers from their necks.

Tommy pulled his supplies out of his sacks, except for the Unknowns bags. He didn't touch those. "So what's this camp like?" Tommy looked at the stepbrothers.

Quid turned to Blake and snickered. "Let's just say a bit unpredictable. I don't care where you went to camp before, you're in for some big surprises. Best you find out for yourself. Everybody's schedule is different and changes all the time, too. Be sure to check your computer print-out every morning."

Tommy smiled nervously. *Surprises can be good or bad. I hope mine are good.* He studied Blake pondering how he might sketch him in his Red Notebook.

Quid noticed his gaze. "There's something you need to know about my brother," Quid said to Tommy. "He's got this thing, maybe because I was born first, and he was second," Quid paused. "You tell him Blake."

Tommy turned toward Blake. He wasn't sure he wanted to hear but asked politely, "What is it?"

"Get it out," Quid ordered Blake, dropping onto the revolving sofa across the room.

"Simply that I've got to be first. I hate to wait. I'm telling you, I need to be up front in every line. I sometimes have to knock guys down to get there. I'm sorry. I wish I wasn't like this, but I always want to be first."

Tommy had never heard of anybody needing to be first. He usually tailed along last because he stopped to examine things around him.

"No problem, Blake. You can go on ahead of me much as you want."

Blake rushed over to pump Tommy's hand again. "Thanks."

"Unless it's a competition," Tommy added, "then, of course, I have to do my best."

Blake's face fell.

Quid whooped and climbed on Piney's bed and started jumping on the mattress.

"Hey, guy, what are you doing?" Piney yelled. "This is my bed, not a trampoline."

"Sorry," Quid said. He hopped to the floor and started doing jumping jacks.

"Then there's my brother," Blake said clapping his hands in the air then pointing in Quid's direction. "If you think I'm weird, look at him! Quid can't sit still. He's always jumping or running back and forth. Talk to him and he doesn't even hear you. Sometimes I think he doesn't even know where he is."

"I keep moving because it helps me think," Quid explained. He started pacing. "Like this." He grinned.

"Jump around somewhere else. We don't like it in here. Do we, Smurlee?" Piney sat up and removed his headphones.

"It's okay by me." Tommy began to stack his books, flashlight, and binoculars on the shelves above his dresser.

"Well I don't like it." Piney glared at Tommy. "How'd I get you for a roommate? I can tell you and I are going to need to get some things straight."

"Now, now," Quid said. "Remember a gentle answer turns away anger."

Piney pointed at Quid. "I call you Quid the Quoter because you're always quoting people alive and dead —a real brain."

"Okay guys, that's enough." Quid had enough of being the center of attention.

Blake turned to Piney. "Then there's Piney. He's okay if you like big baboons."

Piney charged at Blake who scrambled under the bed.

"I can see you guys are a fun bunch. By the way, where'd you get the nickname, Piney?" Tommy wanted to change the subject.

Piney patted his thighs with pride. "My legs are thick and straight like pine tree trunks."

"Yeah, plus bad feelings and grudges stick to him like sap. He's holding one now against Orson Gartini," Blake added crawling out.

"So?" Piney glared at Blake. "I can't help it. That's the way I am. My Dad was the same." Piney bent to play with his lizard.

"No one has to be a way just because their Dad or Mom were," Tommy said quietly.

Piney stared at him. "A lecture? You messing with me, kid?"

"Orson beat Piney out last year for Super Sleuth in Camp Poisons," Blake explained. "But Piney swears Orson cheated."

"He did!"

"Quiet, the door's open. He may hear you," Blake looked nervously over his shoulder toward the door.

Quid began to pace in a slow circle.

"Who's Orson Gartini?" Tommy asked.

"You don't want to know," Blake said.

"A guy I can't stand," Piney explained. "Just keep your guard up. He's around here somewhere, and he's dangerous." Piney clenched his fists.

Tommy said, "I'm not going to be scared of someone I've never met."

"I tell you he's bad news, Smurlee. Whose side are you on?" Piney asked.

"Nobody's. I mean everybody's. Getting along is all I care about." *And I want to crack every code and mystery there is, he thought. That's why I'm here.*

Quid stopped walking long enough to add, "If you want to survive here, stay away from Orson. He'll eat you alive. He likes guys who try to buddy up to him."

Tommy didn't need to hear any more. "What's your lizard's name, Piney?" he asked.

"Zardo. I get to keep a pet in our room, you can't," Piney explained impatiently. "After you pass the Pet Guard and Responsibility Test you get your pick from the lab. Didn't

28

you know that? Who's doing new camper info with you? They didn't tell you anything?"

"You're supposed to be, Piney," Quid informed him. "You're his room mate."

Piney gave Quid a dark look. "See that box next to my lizard's cage, Smurlee?"

Tommy followed Piney's gaze to a white cardboard shirt box.

"It's full of crickets," Piney said. "Don't open it. I feed them to Zardo once a week."

"Speaking of food, let's get dinner," Blake suggested.

"Fine by me," Tommy said.

"Are you going to introduce Tommy to Grella?" Quid asked Piney.

Piney only glared at him. "What do you think?"

"Why is it so bright in here?" Tommy asked when they'd reached the dining hall. He strained his neck tilting his head back. "I've never seen a red ceiling before."

"It's painted Royal Red. I saw the can when they did touch-ups. Somebody squirted mustard up there last summer. The color red is supposed to scientifically stimulate our brains while we eat," Quid said.

"Yeah. The Red Experiment goes for three summers. This is the third one," Blake added munching on a roll.

"No kidding!" Tommy was excited to be in a real life research project. Who knew what sitting underneath intense red three times a day during every meal would do? He didn't think it could do him any harm anyway. Besides, red was his favorite color. His notebook was red, wasn't it? "Who's doing the research?" he asked.

"Counselor Zeller," Piney explained, "every camper also has to spend one afternoon a week in the red chamber listening to accordion music, another brain stimulant, according to a study by Fosdick."

Tommy, Piney, and the Hammond brothers sat at a long table together. A conveyor belt ran down the center of all the tables moving slowly so campers could grab hot food from the shoebox-sized warming ovens and cold stuff from the mini-frigs as it went by. Tommy grabbed fixings for a P & J sandwich, plus an apple, carrots, banana and a lemonade as the conveyor passed. "I like this. What do you call it?" Tommy asked.

"The Quid Express Food Parade. Quid dreamed up the design one night after a mystery maze session during our first year of camp. It took seven months to create and get it moving. He sold the first one to Dunster's the next year." Blake was clearly proud of his brother.

Piney pulled three donuts out of the Sweets section as it passed.

"Piney Putilla never met a donut he didn't love," Quid whispered to Tommy. "It's starting to show, too." Quid pointed at Piney's waist.

"Quit talking about me," Piney growled. "I heard that."

"Piney may be big," Blake said loudly, "but he's still smaller than Orson Gartini. Orson has at least three inches more at the middle and four on top on him."

Tommy shuddered. Mixing with tough, big kids made him nervous because he wasn't huge for his age. *Once I meet Orson, we'll be friends and I'll be fine,* Tommy told himself.

Later that night Tommy e-mailed his grandparents and parents the news of Dunster Day 1. Then he snuggled into bed and slept soundly until 4 a. m. When he awoke he drew designs for conveyor belts in his Red Notebook while waiting for his alarm to go off at 6.

Tommy was too excited to eat breakfast. His first activity session, Dreamology, was about to begin.

Chapter 4
Dreamology

The Dreamology room was filled with cots and computers in cubicles. Two cots were in each roughly eight by nine foot cubicle. All the window shades were pulled down. The light that seeped through was very dim.

Dreamology, what do we do in here? Tommy wondered. Not just sleep, he hoped. That would be boring. Besides he almost never dreamed when he was asleep. Daydreaming while awake —he did that all the time.

Tommy checked his watch. Five more minutes until the session started. Where was the counselor? How do you design a dream?

Quid and Piney had walked over with Tommy because they were in the same session. On the way Tommy made a mental map for his Red Notebook of the way they'd come. He was keeping careful track of directions because this camp was huge. He also intended to record the highlights of each day's activities.

Piney pointed Tommy toward a cubicle. "We're on cots next to each other in here. Before we get started, Smurlee, get this straight. I'm assigned to supervise you the first week only since you're a new camper. But stay out of my way in Dreamology, understand?"

"What could I possibly do to bother you?"

"I'm warning you, don't disturb me, that's final," he said gruffly. "I'm working on a masterpiece of a dream that I started last year. In it I'm the Sportstar of the Century. Last year I had 30 points every basketball game, 10 hits and at least three homers every baseball game. I've broken three of Tiger Wood's golf records, and my tennis serves are always aces. Today I'm hoping to add three goals per soccer game. And win a bicycle race, Le Tour de France. Don't disturb me!"

Tommy struggled to keep his patience. Piney could talk nicer to him. "Where's the counselor?" Tommy asked.

"Counselor Wishkowski is always late for everything. We always started without him last summer. Get set on your cot."

"Are you sure? I don't know what to do yet. I mean what if I fall back asleep?"

"You're supposed to!"

"I'm not trained."

"How will you ever learn if you don't start? I'll direct you."

"Okay."

Tommy and Piney stretched out side by side on twin-size beds. Tommy immediately sat up again and punched his pillow into a comfy shape for his head. Piney reached over and snatched the pillow away.

"No pillows," Piney ordered. "They can make dreams wavy and sometimes downright bumpy."

"Are you sure?"

"I've tried it. Now start thinking of the place you'd like to go."

"A place? That's easy. I'd like to go to Africa to see my parents."

"Fine."

"What if I end up in the wrong place?"

"Like the middle of the Sahara desert? You might.   I almost died of thirst there last year."

Tommy must have looked shocked, because Piney added, "Not really, but it took me three days to stop craving water. Dreaming is so real. Make yourself dream as specifically as possible."

"But how? On second thought, maybe I'll wait until the Counselor comes." Tommy started to get out of bed.

Piney grabbed his arm.

"You'll be fine," Piney said. "This is a controlled dream. Now get back down on your cot. Don't get us in trouble with Counselor Wishkowski."

Tommy settled back. He wanted to dream about his parents but decided to take whatever dream he got. Trust, trust, he muttered to himself. To his surprise, sleep came quickly.

Suddenly the cubicle seemed to sway. Blue and yellow lights lit up a big billboard over his head. The word Dreamscape in giant letters appeared. Was he dreaming or awake? Ten minutes passed, peaceful, refreshing.

Then Tommy felt himself sliding toward a giant barn filled with something soft and sloppy like pudding. A red light started to blink and another message popped out of nowhere. "Go backwards."

He heard a firm voice saying, "Don't stop. We've got to get through this. Fear will block the way for sure. Relax."

"But there's a red light."

"No! Go!"

In the next instant Tommy roared through the pudding in reverse.

Tommy's dream slowed as the light softened to a lighter purple. He passed a man and a boy who were drifting together in space talking. They said something to him as he passed, but he couldn't make it out. The words of their sentences were arranged backwards. His brain couldn't switch them fast enough. The old man shook his head no and pointed his finger.

Tommy figured it was a warning. Of what? The soft purple light disappeared and Tommy was in total blackness for almost a minute. A door opened letting light in. He found himself in some kind of corral. He could hear loud animals' hooves, maybe buffalo, coming closer. Omigosh! They were heading straight for him.

Piney's voice vibrated around him, "Get out of there. Dream different! Think Dreamology Lab!"

Seconds later Tommy yelled "Avalanche."

Piney bolted from his bed and rushed over to Tommy. "Wake up!"

Tommy muttered sleepily, "Watch out. Take cover. There are millions of rocks dropping from the mountain. I'm up there falling with them."

"Wake up! You're having a nightmare!"

"No, we've got to stop the barrage of blue marbles. They're hard rubber ones, not rocks, I see."

It took several shakes before Piney could wake Tommy.

Finally Tommy lifted his head and looked at Piney.

"You just totally messed up my dream!" Piney's face was bluish red.

"I did? I'm sorry." Tommy insides felt like popcorn kernels shaking in a pot. He tried to get up and fell off the cot.

"Sorry! You're sorry!" Piney's arms were straight as sticks, fists clenched. "You woke me up twice! You ruined my dream sequence! Do you know what happens when you're awakened more than once in the middle of a dream? You can never get it back again. A dream must be allowed to move to completion. It's the only way it can get into permanent memory! Do you know how long I've worked to perfect my sports star dream series? Now what?"

"I said I'm sorry."

"There's no need to repeat yourself. I'm angry, not stupid."

"Okay, okay." Tommy was getting annoyed too, now. "I told you I shouldn't do this without training. Go back to sleep. Maybe you'll dream something better."

"Something better. Fat chance."

"Oh stop it." Tommy's hands were sweating and he was still shaking from his dream.

Piney noticed and started to calm down a little. Maybe he could add another sport to the mix and try again for a new dream. He got back in his bed and looked over. "Maybe I was a little hard. You're supposed to record the results when you wake up —the images, ideas, that stuff. It goes on your computer. Not bad actually for your first time, Smurlee. At least you went somewhere."

"But I was out of control totally."

"I figured you were. That's why I woke you."

"Thanks."

"Grella did the same for me when I was getting started," Piney said. "We'll try again tomorrow.

"Who's Grella?"

Piney didn't answer. He squashed the pillow over his head and didn't say another word until the end of the period.

When the buzzer sounded Quid awoke drowsily from his bed down the line. He stopped by Tommy's cubicle on his way out.

"Smurlee, how did it go?"

"I had a little problem with my first dream."

"Watch out, The Mean Machine, Orson Gartini has Dreamology, too. I don't know why he's not here in Dream Lab. Maybe he's still getting settled. He likes to slip into the cubicle of new campers and mess with their computers. Whatever you do don't let him in your cubicle."

"How can I keep him out?"

Quid shrugged. "You better!"

"What makes this Orson so mean?"

"He continually feeds his brain the poison of bitterness. Have you ever known someone who never forgets any bad thing anybody ever said or did to him? Even if you just remind him of another kid he doesn't like, you're in trouble. That's Orson. He thrives on destroying anything or anyone."

"Great. I had enough trouble in here dreaming on my own."

"Forget about him now. This session is over. C'mon, let's get a game up of Wicket Thicket." Quid led the way to the East Field.

Piney, Quid and Tommy joined a group of other players already out there.

"Hey, Grella, c'mere," Piney said.

Tommy watched as a girl of about ten or eleven strolled over. Her eyes, big and brown, had a look of constant wonder.

"What's happening?" Grella pulled off her headphones and fluffed her long blonde hair. She saw Tommy and asked, "Who's this?"

"My new roommate."

"Pleased to meet you." Tommy stuck out his hand to shake hers.

"Same here," Grella said. "I was listening to a lecture on bugs while waiting for the game to start."

"Grella's the only camper who slid through Mystery Substances with all A's and scarcely opened the book. If you need to do teamwork with someone, choose her," Quid whispered.

Tommy noticed a clear plastic box with holes punched into it dangling from Grella's belt loop. It was jiggling. "What's that hooked on your belt?"

"My pet grasshopper. He goes with me everywhere. His name is Fletcher. He's my third bug pet. Orson ate one of the other two. He's so mean!"

"You're kidding?" Tommy was amazed.

"No, he eats bugs for snacks. I hate him."

"Hate's a strong word," Tommy said.

"Not for him." Grella threw her head back. "And he's got evil friends who do what he says, too, and he's buddies with Dagta. He's the worst of all."

Tommy squirmed. Her words gave him a sick feeling in his stomach. He didn't even like thinking about people who liked to hurt others and he sure didn't want to be around them. "Whatever *is good, pure and true, think on that*, Tommy reminded himself.

"His power sounds so dark. How does he get people to follow his evil plans?" Tommy asked.

"Captures their thoughts with lies," Grella said matter-of-factly. "Once he gets into your thoughts, he can get into your dreams, too."

"How do I stop him?"

"Keep thinking about something good, pure and true. It's the best way."

Tommy looked at her amazed. "That's what I just told myself."

"Smart," she said.

"Time for warm-ups before the game," Piney ordered.

"Piney's made himself the captain, of course." Grella laughed. "One more thing," she added, "when you're in group activities, Tommy, don't let Orson get close." Then she took off after Piney down the field.

Tommy shuddered, planning to keep Orson as far away as the North Pole. He went back to his room to finish unpacking. Plenty of time for games later. He wanted to get settled in. He didn't know Piney had other plans.

Chapter 5
The Great Mystery Plan

Piney returned from the game and blurted out, "Hey Smurlee, I called a Dorm Wing Meeting in our room tonight." Piney said it as casually as if this could happen every night. The Hammond brothers followed him in and began a chess game at the corner table.

Tommy looked up from what he was reading. He struggled to stay calm and avoid arguing in front of the Hammond brothers. It wasn't easy. After all this was his room, too. He should have been asked. Piney and he would be having a talk about this and soon.

By 8 p.m. Blake, Quid, Toodle, Grella, Molar and Maryna Malone had gathered. Tommy had never seen the Malones before. Quid introduced them. "Maryna's the youngest camper," Quid said.

"Hi," Tommy said politely. "How old are you, Maryna?"

"Not telling unless you tell first."

"I'm twelve," Tommy said shaking his head and sitting down in the circle the campers formed on the carpet.

"Nine and a half. I hope we win! I hate to lose." Maryna plopped down on the floor. She tugged on a strand from her chin-length brown hair that was as straight as a broom and about the same color.

"I do too."

"Even though she's not yet ten, Maryna's allowed to come to camp because her brothers Molar and Groaner Malone are both here," Grella said.

For a few minutes the group chatted about activities. Then Piney stood and said, "Listen up. We're here to plan our strategy."

Piney glared at Tommy, then Molar who were talking about their experiences in Dreamology. "Quiet, especially you newcomers."

Mr. Toodle straightened to his full height, "Remember your manners, Mr. Putilla."

"I will, never you mind." Piney looked around to be sure he had everyone's full attention. "Now as some of you know the highlight of every summer at Dunster's Camp of Mystery and Inventions is the Great Unsolved Mystery Challenge. Every dorm wing becomes a team. We've got seven clues to find. Look around at the people who will be our team of seven with Molar as an alternate."

No one said a word. Piney was big, tough, and sounded confident. Everyone was glad to have Piney on the team, except Mr. Toodle who thought he was rude. Good manners were important to Mr. Toodle.

"A win, pure and simple, that's what I'm after. It's a fine thing to have a win at Dunster's," Piney said. "Plus life doesn't get any sweeter than besting Gartini and his honchos. Who's with me on this?"

"That's what I want, too!" Tommy announced coolly.

"Solving this great unsolved mystery will be easy," Molar said.

Everybody stared at him. Tommy hadn't met Molar before.

Molar had a big mouth and chunky, square teeth. His face looked like it was all mouth. His hands and feet were huge too, but the rest of him was normal eleven-year-old size.

"Hey! This mystery is no easy camp exercise, it's hard work!" Quid warned Molar. "And tricky! Thirty per cent of the time the Dunster mysteries are never solved."

"What happens to them then?" Molar wanted to know.

"They get put into the file of great unsolved mysteries."

"That's not going to happen this year." Tommy spoke confidently.

"Now I called you together," Piney said, "because we have to decide before tomorrow who will lead our team? I'm the most qualified."

Quid said, "I already know who I'd pick."

But all seven had to agree.

Blakely started to say "Quid" when Piney slapped him hard on the back.

Grella shouted "Tommy!"

"Aye," Blake said instantly.

"Aye," Molar repeated.

"Yes," Quid said.

One after another all seven people were in agreement. Tommy would lead them.

Tommy looked around amazed and flattered. He offered modestly, "Piney, you're older and more experienced."

"I can't," Piney said, "Don't let it get your head. I'd lead, but my Dad was on the Camp Board so I'm not allowed to be an official leader." He smirked at Tommy. "But I can lead through you."

Tommy cringed. So this was his plan. That would not be alright with him. "Sorry to disappoint you, Piney," he said, "but that won't work. If I have the title, leader, I'm responsible for what happens. I need to make final decisions."

"Wrong kid, I give the orders here." Piney pulled out his cell phone and ignored Tommy.

Tommy stood up. "Then you'll need to find another leader."

"Oh yeah, well what if I say different? Listen, kid, don't push me."

Tommy's fingers started to shake. "No one's pushing you." Tommy put his hands behind his back. He tossed his shoulders back and stretched to his full height. "Piney, if I lead. I'm in charge. Understood?"

"We need to have a discussion, outside, right now." Piney stomped toward the door.

Tommy knew he meant a fight. Tommy's forehead beaded with sweat. "I won't fight you. That's dumb. We need to work together to succeed. No one should get all the credit, not the leader or anyone. A team does the work, a team gets the win, but I do the leading. A leader leads." Tommy was praying silently even as he spoke. "Anyone who wants to be on my team line up behind me!"

Piney watched as first Blakely, Grella, Maryna, then Quid, and Toodle, all formed a row behind their leader. Molar hesitated then agreed. Piney growled, "Okay. Save me a spot."

Grella, ever the peace person, said, "Now that that's settled, we need a counselor to be our sponsor. How about Counselor Artur?"

Quid jumped in, "I like him – he's a medieval mystery expert. Last year he was a big help to his team. He could be a plus for us."

"Fine by me. I think the medieval time period is nifty," Blake said.

"Who cares?" Piney turned and stalked out of the room.

Tommy dropped onto a chair. He had established his authority.

"He'll get over it," Grella whispered to Tommy, "that was great. Now if you can stand up to Orson Gartini and Dagta, we're in business. They're the biggest problems."

"Who's Dagta?" Tommy asked.

"Orson's demonic super power. He'll use Dagta to cheat and try to steal any clues he can't find himself. Orson won two years ago using Dagta, but nobody could prove it."

"I thought Dunster's Rules of Mystery Solving forbade the use of any demonic assistance," Quid said.

"That's right," Blake pulled out red licorice sticks from a pencil length pocket stitched just below his knee. He passed them around to everyone. "Asking angelic protection is acceptable under Rule 3 of play, but no demons, no tarot cards, no psychic interventions."

Quid put a finger to his lips, "Not so loud, these things aren't even to be talked about. They are used to let demons in. Too many kids end up demon influenced."

Grella nodded gravely. "Even the use of angels has rules. Angels can never be requested by name. You can only ask for angelic help through the Sunmaker. He makes all the decisions about angels - who, where and when they help."

Tommy said, "Fine by me. The Sunmaker gives me help when I need it. He may be invisible, but He's there when you need Him. I can hear His voice within me wherever I go."

Maryna turned to Toodle. "The exciting thing is that tomorrow the Great Unsolved Mystery starts and we have our team ready."

"And we're going to win!" Toodle made a fist in the air.

"Providing Piney co-operates," Blake added.

"He better," Grella said, "or else."

Chapter 6
Tunnel Trouble

"Assemble in the Great Hall for the official beginning of this year's Great Unsolved Mystery!" Croggle's announcement came over the audio system.

At 3 p.m. eight teams clustered in groups of seven in the large hall usually used to display camper inventions. Piney, the twins, Grella, Maryna, Toodle and Tommy sat together at one table.

Director Croggle stood at the table in front of the room. He pompously opened the chest next to him, pulled out a paper and began to read stretching out his words: "Mystery Number 37 begins tonight. Remember as you conduct your investigations you must continue with your regular camp sessions. Mystery solving is to be fitted into designated periods and free time. Any questions?"

No one made a sound so Croggle continued.

"The rules are no spitting, kicking, or jumping on opponents on the premises. When you find a Mystery Card clue it will typically be in an envelope. Select only one from the packet of envelopes. I repeat, take only one, leave the rest for the other teams. Then go to a private place and read the clue with your team. Study it together. Don't destroy the Mystery Card containing the clue! You must be able to prove that you actually went to each clue location. All clue cards will all be collected and shredded at the end. May the best mystery squad be victorious."

A loud cheering followed his words. Quid stomped his feet.

"We can do it!" Piney yelled.

"I can't wait to start!" Grella rubbed her hands together.

"Now, teams, it's my pleasure to announce the person in charge of this year's mystery — Counselor Wudderbuster, a famous man of mystery. He'll give you additional instructions."

Wudderbuster struggled to get his large, round shape out of his chair. Counselor Spindlesticks ran over to help. He gave him a strong tug.

Meanwhile Croggle continued to lead the campers in clapping.

Wudderbuster waddled to the microphone and spread his notes on the podium. "Remember to use caution always, safety first, we've only lost three campers in our thirty-six years of solving mysteries, but we don't want to lose any more." He pulled out his handkerchief to wipe his brow. Getting out of the chair seemed to have tired him.

"Lost? Did they die?" Tommy whispered to Piney and Quid sitting on either side of him.

"One was too ambitious and drowned," Piney said.

"Another got caught under the wheels of a moving car. That was two years ago," Quid whispered back. "No one knows what happened to the third. He disappeared."

"How horrible! Tommy said.

Wudderbuster's crackly voice continued. "Remember there's to be absolute secrecy within your group. Thinking ability is essential, as well as using your imagination. Sometimes the meaning of a clue may be revealed to you during a dream. Always be alert for answers. They may come to you when you least expect it. You have six weeks to solve the mystery. Of course, I expect that you'll solve it sooner, but if, at the last week of week no team has succeeded, the mystery will be declared unsolvable."

Counselor Wudderbuster stopped for a sip of water. "The starting place for all teams and the location of the first clue is, by tradition, the speed tunnel."

Grella poked Tommy and whispered, "It's tough to get through the tunnel, but once you do, you automatically get the clue."

"Shhh, Wudderbuster's still talking." Blake said.

"Everyone on your team must wear a colored band on your wrist or ankle when engaged in the active pursuit of clues. The name of your team will be the name of the color bands you select." He held up a one-quarter inch wide strip of green fabric. "If you find a clue without your wristband on you can't activate it or use the information."

Molar Malone walked among the tables passing out packets of bands from a small plastic bag Counselor Spindlesticks had handed him.

Tommy selected seven silver bands for his team members. He examined his closely. It looked like it might glow in the dark. He didn't trust himself to remember to put his band on daily —he decided he'd never take it off, not even when he showered. Tommy snapped the band around his ankle and pulled his sock up over it.

A prickle of pride trickled through him. As long as this band was attached to his body he was a sleuth. He might be a newcomer, and a bit smaller than some of the other campers, but he was the team leader and he was going to make sure he did everything he could to help his team win.

Dad always said determination doubles your power to do anything, Tommy remembered.

Dad and Mom also taught him to use the Sunmaker's supernatural power. *How many teams know that?* Tommy wondered smugly. Then he caught himself. Feeling cocky and thinking he was superior would dilute the power. He knew better.

A sudden shuffling of chairs sounded then the room began to empty. The teams hurried toward the tunnel. Orson charged to the door. He reached it the same moment as Piney. He used his shoulder like a ram to shove Piney out of the way. Piney gave Orson a body slam back. While the two scuffled Blake slipped around both of them and went out.

Counselor Wudderbuster waddled over and separated the boys. "None of that or I'll disqualify you both from participation!" He sounded really mad.

Grella rushed up with Toodle and together they gently led Piney to a chair and hovered around him until Orson left. "Don't waste your energy. We need your help to get through the tunnel."

Piney mumbled, "You're right."

"Let's catch up with the rest of the team." Grella said, "I want to cheer them on, but no way am I going into the tunnel. It's torturous. I get sick on roller coasters and twister rides."

"This is where we start," Mr. Toodle said leading Tommy, Quid, and Piney to the tunnel entrance in the rear of Counselor Blinkton's room on the lower level.

"Whatchamajigger and his campers devised this tunnel system three years ago," Quid explained. "We went through it last year. It took us days to master the tunnel. We're counting on you to be quicker, Tommy."

"I hope so."

Tommy squinted at the door to the tunnel. A thick mist hovered over it. A sound like pretzels cracking came from inside. "What's that noise?" Tommy asked.

"That's the opening and shutting of the chute into the speed tunnel," Quid said.

Counselor Blinkton wearing a black turtleneck and black pants ran up panting. His hair was dark brown, the same shade as his big egg-shaped glasses. His eyes gleamed with excitement behind the lens. "Blake's been in and out of my room checking the speed tunnel's door since early this morning. He wants to be first. Come in, everyone, for your final instructions." The campers clustered around him.

"Every team will enter from a separate tunnel. This is your initiation into the physical rigors required for mystery work. First you'll walk about twenty feet through a dark tunnel, then go down a two hundred foot speed slide. It will feel like you're falling through outer space. Then comes the tricky part. Getting up and walking through the gigantic moving cylinder made of twenty huge barrels one after the other isn't easy. You must keep your balance until you reach the end. That's where the Mystery Card clue envelopes are. Any questions?"

"Yes. How do we get through?" Toodle joked.

All the campers started talking at once.

"The final part of the tunnel is the hardest," Quid whispered to Tommy, "I never made it. I tried every day last year at camp. I still have a bruised knee from it."

Counselor Blinkton's voice bellowed over the noise. "Silence! Silence!" he yelled. "I'm not finished! When you reach the end, that is, if you reach it, the clue will be visible. Don't linger. Get out quick." Counselor Blinkton stopped speaking, bent over and sneezed.

Tommy stared at the dark hole in the Counselor's mouth. He was missing several teeth.

The Counselor noticed Tommy's gaze and quickly closed his mouth and rubbed his jaw. "I lost them two nights ago when I tried to get through on a practice run. I couldn't get the timing quite right. Now where were we?"

Quid rubbed his finger across his two front teeth and started pacing faster.

Counselor Blinkton waved his arm grandly. "No matter, you're all younger, you'll do fine! Now, at the end of the tunnel, grab a clue envelope. Seven envelopes, one for each team, are taped to the Victory "V".

"Three members, and only three, from each team may try to get through the tunnel to the clue at any one time. Your biggest challenge will be staying out of each other's way. You may alternate team members, as long as one person comes out before a sub goes in and only three are in at any one time. Time is critical. Is everybody ready?"

"When we reach the end how do we get out of the tunnel and back up the speed slide?" Tommy asked.

"Retrace your steps," Blinkton said. "Once you're in position on the slide a blast will shoot you up. Don't try to leave the tunnel area until the buzzer sounds, but you must leave when it does. Must!"

Blinkton passed out small pins with a green glass center that glowed in the dark. "Wear this pin on your sleeve," he instructed. "They're push button. Hold the button down ten seconds to turn it on or off. Only one member of your team may have his light on at any one time."

"Each team leader picks the three campers who go." Blinkton gave a few more instructions and sent them off.

"I want to go in now," Piney said.

"No, Piney, you're first alternate," Tommy ordered. "Quid and Blake will start in with me." Tommy didn't want to deal with Piney's bossiness yet. He tried to soften Piney's disappointment. "You're experienced, Piney, if we miss, you'll get the clue for us."

Blake ran up holding a laundry basket. "Blinkton assigned the tunnelers these special clothes, black shirts and jeans with a black plastic poncho over everything. He says it will help us slide easier."

Blake passed the clothes out and they dressed quickly in their identical outfits.

"Everybody turn on your green glow pin so I can see you," Tommy said.

Tommy turned to his teammates. "Remember if we get separated, try to avoid using your light. Someone else may be using his."

"Right, boss," Piney said sarcastically.

Tommy ignored him. "Okay, Blake you go into the tunnel first. Quid will follow, then me. What's our Dunster's motto, guys?"

"D-I-D-I, dream it, do it!" They high-fived one another.

Blake entered the door of the tunnel.

Tommy could hear Blake's voice becoming more distant.

"I'll be at the speed slide soon, it's just ahead!" Blake said. "Five ya-a-a-rdssss."

"He must be sliding down now," Tommy yelled.

Blake was gone. Not another sound.

"Quid," Tommy said, "go."

Quid looked white and shaky, but he got into position. Then he froze. "I can't do it," he said.

"Sure you can." Tommy expected this might happen. He went behind and gave Quid a solid push.

"Zowwweeeee." Then silence.

Tommy counted to ten then took a deep breath and entered.

Inside the tunnel his eyes gradually adjusted to the darkness, but he couldn't see anyone ahead. Tommy took a few steps cautiously. A cold draft of air blew on his face from somewhere in front of him.

Counselor Blinkton's voice came into the tunnel over the sound system like an echo from a canyon. "Use caution, campers."

Tommy took another step. Then the ground was gone. He fell flat on his back. This had to be the start of the speed slide. He felt for the edges and held his breath. Where were the protective sides? His body rolled like a rubber ball. Tommy had planned to gage his time, but was too scared to think.

He landed on a thick, sticky substance like rubber glue. Instantly a thousand pillow feathers stuck all over his suit. Good thing he was wearing this outfit.

In the distance Tommy heard Blinkton's muffled voice coming over the loud speaker giving more instructions. Was it Blinkton's voice or was Orson playing a trick? Did he get access to the sound system? "Get up, turn, and then slither."

Get up in this huge rounded moving tunnel? How? Tommy wondered. The tunnel never stopped rolling! Tommy was in the giant cylinder moving in fast motion forward, then backward, then sideways. One second he was upside down, then right side up a second and down again! Feathers flew everywhere.

He tried to stand and walk but couldn't. He heard Quid ahead of him, then behind him rolling around and around and sliding into him, almost tripping Tommy when he tried to stand.

Finally Tommy got his footing. Could he master this? He had to stay standing long enough to figure out the tunnel moves mathematically. Tommy counted the number of gyrations and noted the changes of direction the cylinder that occurred every ten seconds. Sideways, backwards and forwards in reverse order each time.

Okay, he thought, *I can do this.*

Just then Quid banged into his backside.

"Hey, Quid," Tommy yelled, "turn on your light and watch out."

"I can't stop."

"Well, then get out so you won't be in my way."

"I'm trying to help you," Quid said.

"Don't!" Tommy got up again and tried to place his feet in a kind of rhythm to go with his math calculations. If only he could get where the motion went steadily forward before the tunnel sucked him back. It was tricky, but he would do it. "Dream It, Do It," he said aloud over and over.

Quid and Piney slid like boomerangs back and forth past him. Why was Piney in here? What had happened to Blake?

Each time Tommy made a little progress. He managed to stand a few seconds longer and walk in deeper. He should be almost to the end of the tunnel if his computations were correct. Had his breathing become heavier or had the air around him become thicker? He struggled to keep his feet from slipping. He couldn't be sure how much time they had left.

Tommy sucked in his breath. He must be close.

Blinkton said no one ever mastered the tunnel the first time through.

It couldn't be much farther. A glimmer of white flickered lighting up a huge "V." The envelopes were just ahead.

Then he heard the warning buzzer. Soon he'd be sucked back up.

"Oh, no. I'm so close." Tommy fought a desire to drop to the ground and moan. One more minute, maybe two.

"Sunmaker, help," Tommy whispered. Whenever he did something really hard, he asked for supernatural help. He had to have more power to lunge. Suddenly, like air releasing from a balloon, Tommy shot to the end of the tunnel, grabbed one of the envelopes and was sucked back to the beginning of the tunnel!

Another blast and he was at the top of the slide and out the tube, just as the final whistle blew.

Tommy dragged himself from the entrance. His clothes were singed and stinking of smoke although he'd never seen any fire. He waved the envelope at Quid.

"You did it!" Quid let out a big cheer.

"Where's everybody?" Tommy asked.

"Blake was the first one out. When he got ejected Piney went in."

"Where's Piney now?"

"Still in there. He didn't come out when the second buzzer sounded."

"What's that terrible smell," Tommy asked.

"It's the friction created by the fast rolling of the speed tube and the people shooting in and out of the speed tunnel," Counselor Blinkton said. He hovered around the opening as the next team went in.

"There's Piney." Blake pointed to a bedraggled figure staggering out of the tunnel. He was gasping and his skin had turned an ugly shade of green.

"Piney, we got the first clue envelope!" Tommy said to cheer him up.

"Yeah, later, I'm sick."

"We know what to do," Quid said. "Spin Piney around over and over to remove the effects of the up and down and sideways trips he made in the speed slide." Tommy grabbed Piney's shoulders while Quid reached for his legs. Together they turned his body round and round.

Finally Piney yelled, "That's enough! Smurlee, did I hear you say you almost made it?" He focused bleary eyes on Tommy.

"I did make it!" Tommy said.

"No kidding!" Piney slapped his knee. "If I wasn't so big I could have gotten there myself. Next time we want quicker results, Smurlee!"

Tommy nodded.

One by one they dumped their black outfits into the big plastic bucket Blake passed. Then Blake dragged the bucket to a metal coffin-size box that resembled a flat old-fashioned stove.

"What's that?" Tommy asked.

Blake shoved the clothes inside.

"A De-Smoker. Don't you know anything?" Piney said demonstrating again that he had absolutely no patience.

They watched the De-Smoker box rock and jerk for three minutes. When the tumbling clothes jiggled to a stop a bright light burst from the machine.

Blake hurriedly opened the De-Smoker. He pulled the clothes out in stacks perfectly folded. They smelled like evergreen.

"Another Dunster invention," Blake confided, "but the camper hasn't been able to market it successfully."

"Why not?" Tommy asked.

"Not enough smoky clothes in homes," Blake said.

Piney and the Hammond brothers gathered around while Tommy ripped open the singed envelope and read the Mystery Card aloud:

"Haze, haze, confusion clear,
History will speak again,
In the Hedge Maze green and near
A Mystery Card you will sight,
But you must only enter at night
When the moon is not full."

Tommy checked his watch. It's time for our next activity. "Let's meet after lunch to plan our entrance to the Hedge Maze," Tommy said.

Chapter 7
Nottingood and The Truth Twist

"Gather closer in front of the TV, campers. You may sit on the floor."

Tommy sighed, *this is crazy —a warm, sunny day and we're sitting in front of this TV watching a video. I hope I'm not going to be bored.*

"Get cozy," Counselor Nottingood said. "Keep your eyes on the screen. Remember the first rule of watching TV or reading is, 'Remember, it's not what you think you read or saw, it's what's I say you saw, and what I tell you to think about what you saw or read.'"

"What is this?" Grella mumbled under her breath.

An announcer dressed in a suit appeared on the screen. He spoke for several minutes about the importance of absolute honesty ending with the words, "Lying is always wrong."

Then a second man in a suit appeared. He announced in a deep voice, "You've just heard why truth can be adjusted to the needs of the situation. Others can tell you what to believe. Is it okay to believe someone who disregards facts, if that person thinks they're doing the right thing? Yes, sometimes it is."

Tommy looked at Blake who was pulling headphones from his lower left leg pocket and only half-listening.

Tommy shook his head bewildered. "They're saying different things."

Counselor Nottingood hurried over. "Put that CD player away, Quid Hammond. Watch this show with the rest of the campers."

"Yes, Counselor." Blake poked Tommy and whispered, "Just be quiet, we'll be out of here soon enough. Then we can forget this gobbleygook."

"So why are we watching this if it's not important?" Tommy whispered back.

"It's supposed to be, I mean, they think it is, but you know it's not. They must know too."

"That's the most bizarre thing!" Tommy said.

"Shh, Nottingood's looking at us."

Tommy raised his hand. "Counselor Nottingood, I'm sorry sir, but I'm confused. The first speaker said total honesty is important and told us why, but the next announcer just said honesty isn't important."

"No, my boy, he told you lying is okay." Counselor Nottingood turned to the other campers. "Now we'll write down why lying is okay under certain circumstances."

The campers busied themselves grabbing paper and pens from the stacks Nottingood provided.

"Then absolute honesty isn't important?" Tommy asked.

"Get to work!" Counselor Nottingood held up his hand to stop Tommy's questions.

"But which is it?" Tommy asked frustrated.

Everyone around Tommy ignored him and started writing.

"Mr. Smurlee, it's quite simple. Always speak the truth, but at times you may lie," Counselor Nottingood said turning the pages of the big book on the stand in front of him.

"I'm sorry, Counselor, but I have to disagree. You can't do both!"

"You're sorry, Mr. Smurlee! You choose to disagree with me?" Nottingood turned his back on Tommy. His eyes swept the room. "Listen, campers. Camper Smurlee thinks he's right and all of you are wrong!"

A tittering went across the room.

Counselor Nottingood continued. "It's your opinion, only your opinion about truth, truth changes with need."

"But," Tommy gulped, "that doesn't make sense. I believe the facts show the truth. They don't change."

Nottingood interrupted him. "No, you're misinterpreting. Campers do you hear him?" Nottingood mocked.

The campers' soft trickle of laughter became a roar.

"But, sir, truth is truth," Tommy said. He felt embarrassed at being singled out, but refused to let this stop him.

"Do you presume to know more than the rest of these campers?" Counselor Nottingood gave a loud harrumph. "Even more than me!" He patted his chest with his hand.

"Not more, sir, but I do see this situation differently."

A tiny voice near Tommy in the back of the room, spoke. It was Grella. "Counselor Nottingood," she said, "I believe Tommy Smurlee is right. I agree with him about truth."

"That does it, now there's two of you!" The Counselor exclaimed. He turned to the other campers, "What do the rest of you think?"

The campers began to boo.

"Alright, campers, back to your writing. You, too, Grella Weller and Thomas Surly," the Counselor strutted over to where they were sitting.

"My name is Tommy Smurlee, sir."

"Contradicting me again?" The Counselor's face contorted into an ugly shape.

"I beg your pardon."

"I've had enough. Out, out with both of you." He almost shoved them toward the door.

"Be in my office at exactly 1:00 p.m. I will deal with you then."

Tommy gulped.

Grella cowered against Tommy as they left. "Right is right, I don't care what he says! Let's go have lunch."

"I keep rethinking what happened. But I know I said the right thing. I hope I won't be sent home from camp."

"You said what you had to."

"I did and I'd say it again."

"Well you probably will have to," Grella said, "at 1 p.m." Halfway down the hall she straightened. "I'm not going to let this upset me."

"That's the spirit."

After lunch Tommy and Grella stood in Counselor Nottingood's office on the fifth floor waiting for him to arrive. Tommy hoped he wouldn't be sent home. He really wanted to stay at Dunster's.

The Counselor bustled in. "Sit down," he barked. "Do you realize what you've done?"

Tommy shrugged.

Grella sat silently staring at her wrists.

The Counselor closed the door and took a seat across from them.

Suddenly he smiled. "Congratulations you'll get Ataway ribbons during our closing ceremony at the end of camp, both of you! No one has mastered my session this quickly. I'm quite impressed. I never can tell in advance who will stand for truth. Sometimes it's the most unlikely campers."

"That's all we had to do?" Tommy was confused. "Insist that truth was truth and black was not white?"

"All? Oh no! You did much more than that. You stood for what was right even when everyone around you accepted

58

falseness! Why? Because they don't think for themselves! You had the wisdom to know what was right and the courage to speak up alone to support it."

Grella was still trying to sort out Counselor Nottingood's words. "You mean we're not in trouble?"

"No, no. You were magnificent, but you must keep our secret now. Don't tell anyone at camp why you no longer attend my session. Let them think you had a schedule change." He rubbed his hands together. "I want them to figure this out for themselves."

"But we can't lie, Counselor," Tommy said. "That would go against everything we said in your session."

"You don't need to lie, tell your friends you had a schedule change. You never need to reveal all the facts unless you're being questioned by someone in authority."

Tommy nodded. "That's right. I can do that. Grella, this is great! We now have one extra hour per day to work on Dunster's Great Unsolved Mystery!"

Grella's smile was almost as long as the brim of her baseball cap.

The Counselor rose. "May I shake both of your hands before you leave."

"Certainly sir, thank you," Grella said.

Chapter 8
The Hedge

"Reread the Mystery Clue Card, Quid," Tommy ordered. He and the rest of the Silver team were gathered in the lounge of the West Wing during their break time after lunch.

"Haze, haze, confusion clear,
History will speak again."

"Stop right there. History! That's it!" Quid yelled. "Let's go to the camp archives on the fifth floor where Filey is and read the records of the previously solved mysteries. We'll check the references to the hedge maze before we attempt to go in."

Maryna tugged on Grella. "What are archives?"

"Like a library that houses materials from the past," Grella answered.

"I'd rather go swimming," Maryna said.

"We will, later," Grella said.

"A sensational idea." Blake was ready to start down the hall.

"Possibly this will help," Toodle said, "but the next part of the clue says, 'In the hedge maze green and near, a Mystery Card you will sight,' so I'm not sure we have to bother with the library."

"Checking the archives is a stupid plan." Piney was quick to give his opinion. "I say let's go into the hedge maze as soon as it's night."

"Wait a second! Heading blindly into the maze could be dangerous. It's worse than being lost in a cornfield. A Dunnie went in last year and didn't find his way out for two days," Quid said.

"Are you kidding?" Tommy gulped.

"It's true. We sent search parties in for him," Grella explained, "and lost one of the campers from the search parties, too, for almost thirty-six hours."

"No sweat, stop trying to scare the Silver Team leader. This clue will be easy," Piney said. "Go in, investigate, get out. I could find this clue by myself tonight with both eyes closed."

"Easy! Are you nuts?" Blake looked shocked. "Scratches, pain, think disinfectant, bandages, infirmary. You don't just walk up and go in and out of the hedge maze. You need training in bush diving. And you should only enter at night because that's when the branches soften and separate a tiny bit, otherwise it's too hard to penetrate."

Quid, deep in thought, was pacing the length of the room. He stopped long enough to quote: "Courage is fear that has said its prayers. I say let's pray and go."

"You pray," Piney said. "I'll go in."

Grella shook her head clearly annoyed. "You dove in last year, Piney, and spent the rest of the month in the infirmary. Someone else should go. Who?"

Everyone looked at Tommy.

It was true his mastery of the speed tunnel had led them to the hedge clue days before the other teams. But Tommy wasn't planning to be the one investigating every clue. That didn't sound smart. If he got lost for several days, who would direct the others? These were thinking clues too. Would they be able to handle them?

Still he wanted to keep the girls and Toodle away from the dangers of the hedge. Tommy made his decision. "We'll split into two groups." He had to use his team members wisely.

Tommy assigned Blake, Grella, Maryna and Toodle to the archives for research. "The rest of us will grab some sleep for what may be an all-nighter in the hedge."

"No moon tonight," Quid said after checking the Farmer's Almanac from his back pocket.

Piney started to say, "Splitting up is the dumbest idea I ever heard," but Mr. Toodle coughed so loud no one could hear him anyway. Then Toodle whispered loudly in Piney's ear, "You're not the leader of the Silver Team."

Piney mumbled something no one could hear, then Toodle shut up.

"You'll have time to get a nap at the beach," Tommy told Piney. They agreed to meet at the hedge at nine. Piney stomped out.

"Blake, come back before nine to tell us what you found out at the library," Tommy said.

"Okay. I'll lead the way." Blake strode toward the door. "Follow me to the library, one by one. Don't let anyone see us leave."

"Right," Grella said, "we don't want to be seen by Orson's team or they'll know where the tunnel clue sent us."

"I'm going to the beach," Quid announced.

Tommy put his arm on Quid to hold him back. "I need you with me now."

"Why? We're not going in until dark."

"We'll start by getting an aerial view," he said.

"How do we do that?" Quid asked, "I suppose you have a private helicopter."

"I wish," Tommy said. "We'll check out the maze from the attic floor."

They hurried to the Wind Whoosher and rode it up.

The view from the attic window made Tommy gulp.

The hedge maze was stretch of shrubbery as far as he could see with thistles and brambles. The only sign of activity near it were some blackbirds hovering over a black birdbath at the south end.

"It looks like it goes on half of forever," Quid said. And it did.

"Okay, I've seen enough from here. Let's climb down the fire escape. Keep your eyes on the hedge as we go down. Maybe we can find a good spot to enter by eye-balling it from up here."

"That's a great idea. I don't think anyone ever tried this before." Quid was impressed.

Tommy opened and closed the door to the fire escape slowly so it wouldn't make any noise.

Except it did.

Counselor Nottingood had ears like a hunting dog. He came racing out of his office to the Fire Escape Exit and opened the door. He spotted Tommy and Quid going down the steel ladder and yelled, "What are you doing?"

Tommy thought what he was doing was obvious. Perhaps the counselor should have asked "Why?" Knowing what question to ask is critical, Mom and Dad always said.

The Counselor started down the ladder after them.

"We're getting some fresh air and having a bit of a climb," Tommy yelled to Nottingood, who was quickly descending.

A big gust of wind roared. Tommy and Quid strained to hang on.

Nottingood was wearing a light jacket. The wind caught it and puffed the fabric up into an air balloon.

Nottingood's feet left the rungs of the ladder completely. Tommy watched the Counselor sway from side to side. His arms hung onto the rail with all his strength. Then the wind died as fast as it had come up. Nottingood slammed back against the ladder.

The Counselor changed his mind about coming down further after that.

"Oh alright, go on, go on," the Counselor yelled. "I enjoy a good climb myself now and then, but not in this wind. Next time get my permission first!" He howled the last, climbed back up and went inside.

"Okay," Quid yelled back.

Tommy and Quid continued down busily scanning the hedge for any flecks of white or a bright color. The Mystery Card clue envelope could be wired to a branch. In the tunnel Tommy hadn't needed to hunt for the Mystery Card Envelope. All he had to do was get through the tunnel. Might the hedge clue be visible?

They didn't see anything that looked like it could be an envelope.

Tommy and Quid reached the ground. The cool fresh air made the leaves crackle underfoot.

Piney was waiting for them down below, laughing. "I said this would be easy, but it would be plain stupid to expect the clue to be visible from up there."

"I told you to meet us at the hedge tonight."

"So? I came to check on you. You're my room mate."

"Piney, if you want to stay on this team, you'll follow orders."

"Yeah, yeah. Let's play some basketball then go get dinner, we're having my favorite —pig's feet and boiled cabbage with corn bread. Second choice is cheeseburgers and fries."

"Cheeseburger, cabbage and corn bread for me," Tommy said.

"Sounds like hedge-hunting grub to me," Piney said.

Quid shivered. He wasn't eager for night to fall.

After dinner Tommy returned to his room. His Mom made the best corn bread in the world. What he'd eaten tonight had been nowhere near as good. This mystery and dream work was great. Yet he still had moments when he missed his parents and grandparents. Grandma e-mailed every other day and his parents whenever they could get to an Internet Cafe.

Tommy really wanted news from his family before he went into this hedge maze. He didn't mind admitting to himself he was a little scared. He muttered a prayer before he turned on his computer and went on-line.

Great! He had Mail! He clicked right on.

"Dearest Son,

Your exciting camp activities and new friends sound wonderful.

Dad and I are still in Rwanda researching the silverback mountain gorillas. Their scent is a little like skunk and vinegar, only very light. When we find one, we fall to the ground and approach very cautiously, careful never to get between a silverback and any gorilla babies. The big adults weigh as much as 400 pounds.

Dad learned the gorilla 'hello'. It sounds like a double-belch. The gorillas let us come quite close, but when they want us to go they give a kind of cough grunt that sounds a little like a train starting up. We quickly crawl away backwards when we hear it. Today we sat with a family of eight gorillas for several hours.

Enough about us. How special that you're the leader of your team. We're proud of you. Loved your drawings of the camp and your new friends. Please be careful.

Don't forget your prayers. You're in ours daily, precious. Love, Mom and Dad."

Tommy printed out two copies of the e-mail. He put one copy in his Red Notebook and carefully folded the other into a tiny rectangle that he put it in his pocket. Mom said be careful. The hedge maze sounded menacing. He opened his copy of the Book of Holy Words to read. Then, while he waited for darkness, he thought through his plan.

The hedge-hunting team met at the hedge promptly at nine p.m. —all except for Piney.

"Where is Piney?" Tommy asked clearly annoyed. "He shows up when he shouldn't and is missing when we need him!"

They looked at one another blankly. Nobody knew.

Quid handed Tommy a map. "Here are the parts of the maze I remember. Of course the landscaper could have shaped it differently this year."

"Okay, first let's investigate and see what we're up against." Tommy touched a branch of the hedge. "This branch is green and alive, Quid, but it feels hard like solid metal. Any idea what it's made of?"

"Don't know." Quid shrugged. "But I was in there once. I can give you some pointers. It's not your average row of bushes. This hedge is as wide as a block and solid as a thicket."

"Ouch." A bramble drew blood from Tommy. He blinked rapidly.

Quid watched him. "Interesting aren't they, tiny, thorny, and covered with a slick coating that sticks to your fingers."

Tommy raised himself on his tiptoes so he could peer over the hedge. As he did the hedge inched upwards.

"Look, it's growing! Cool." Tommy couldn't take his eyes off it. The hedge grew at least two inches taller as Tommy raised two inches on his toes. Tommy tried jumping up to

66

see over, but the hedge stayed always just over his head. "How does it do that?" Tommy asked.

"Do what?" Quid asked.

"Keep growing just higher than my eyes?"

"There's a sensor system when you get within a foot of it, that raises the root structure when any solid substance moves into the sensor area. Quite clever, isn't it?" Quid said.

Suddenly Blake appeared. Grella ran up behind him flapping her arms. Maryna and Toodle were with her.

"You're not supposed to be here!" Tommy said.

"I know, but Tommy, the bird!"

"Quiet, we don't want to be seen."

"But listen! It's a bird. Dead! I saw it, now it's gone."

"Birds die all the time," Tommy said.

"But this one had its head twisted off," Grella panted.

"Who would do such a thing?" Tommy said truly shocked.

"We don't know," Toodle said.

"We wanted to warn you," Maryna said. "We think Orson's out of the tunnel."

Toodle nodded. "Orson could pop over any minute." Toodle dreaded meeting Orson anywhere.

A loud horn blasted.

"It's time for bedtime snack and lights out. The rest of you go back," Tommy ordered.

Grella gave a sudden shout. An opening the size of a beach ball appeared in the hedge. With that she turned and dove in.

Tommy yelled, "Grella, wait." But she was gone. She'd vanished instantly. The steel-like teeth of the hedge clamped shut behind her.

"I want to go with Grella," Maryna said. Quid scooped her up to hold her back. "One girl in at a time."

A voice like a foghorn followed. "Quid, Quidley Hammond, report to the Director's office immediately."

"Now what's that about?" Quid groaned.

Tommy tugged on Quid's arm. "Go find out! And bring Maryna back to the dorm. She should never have come. Go! I can't leave Grella."

"You're right," Quid said. "Tommy, you and Blake are the only ones. Do it!" He grabbed Maryna's hand and took off with her.

"Grella won't come out the same place she went in," Blake said. "I'll run to the other end to watch for her."

"What good will that do? She could be in there for hours," Tommy yelled, but Blake was gone.

Tommy's felt like turtles were squirming in his stomach. He took a last look at the hedge, then dove.

Chapter 9
Thunking

The session on Orderly Thunking was rarely boring and certainly not this Wednesday. Counselor Zeller, a tall, muscular counselor, was already barking out directions.

Quid looked at Blake when he walked in late. His lips silently shaped the words, "Are Tommy and Grella back?"

Blake shrugged and took his seat across the room.

"Campers, find a partner and arrange these events in order, the battles of the American Revolution, Civil War and World War I and II. Then you may use the equipment and costumes in here to play a war game, but re-enact it factually."

Quid dragged out two bags of Union and Confederate soldiers and a large plastic layout of the northern and southern states. While they relived the battles Zeller walked around and lectured, "Remember, thunking is like thinking with "U" in it. That means "U" must put yourself into your thoughts. What does this mean? To begin put your thoughts in ORDER, always order! Order first and order last, but the middle sometimes, only for a short time, may hold a bit of disorder. The goal is to order your surroundings and order your mind!" Maps are excellent examples of order. Study them often.

"That reminds me, there's a popular legend at Dunster's—only legend of course —that there's a Hidden Garden somewhere in the gardens on the grounds. Don't try looking for it, because it's not on the map. It may not even exist."

"What does that have to do with order?" Blake whispered to Quid.

"Orderly thinking is based on facts!" Every camper's eye focused on Counselor Zeller, who was pulling on one edge of his huge black mustache. He stared at the top of their heads, began to stutter and cough, then halted to clear his throat.

Quid edged forward on his seat.

The campers were worried that he'd stopped, but he went on more quickly.

"You may choose to believe this but I assure you it's totally without a basis in fact. As an O.T.—my initials for Orderly Thunker —you know the importance of fact. Spell it campers, f-a-c-t." He reeled around and wrote the word on an old blackboard leaning against the wall.

When he turned back to the group, all the lights in the room flickered off and on. Then they went off and came on again. Counselor Zeller started perspiring. The lights flickered again.

"This session is over," Zeller announced dismissing the campers twenty minutes early.

"Hey, we didn't finish our games," Quid complained as they filed out.

"What was that all about?" Blake asked.

"Something strange is going on with this guy," Quid said, "That's all I know. Maybe it has something to do with the great mystery."

Tommy staggered back to his room later that day just before bedtime. His tee shirt was torn and he had green streaks all over his shorts.

Piney was resting on his bed.

"How'd you get out of the hedge?" Piney asked.

"Thanks for being concerned." Tommy flopped on his bed. "How long did you look for me?" Tommy asked.

"I had activities all day today. Besides I knew it was hopeless."

"You're probably right." Tommy let out a deep sigh. "It's worse than a jungle in there."

Piney knocked on the adjoining wall for Blake and Quid to come.

"I never saw Grella," Tommy told them. "I couldn't find her inside the maze. I don't know if she ever got out. I've been looking all this time. Finally I found an opening and took it. Is she back?"

Blake said, "I watched the entrance for about an hour. Nobody came out. I waited as long as I could."

Before you got bored, Tommy thought.

"I went back after lunch today and got lucky," Blake said with a big grin. "Just as I was about to leave, Grella popped out with barely a scratch on her."

"Heaven forbid you should have to practice patience," Blake's stepbrother Quid said.

"Why would I want to practice something I hate?"

"Why do you hate it?" Quid asked. "You need it."

"Not now, forget the lecture," Blake said turning away. "Excuse me, Piney, will you get Grella please?"

Blake turned to Tommy. "Cheer up, Tommy, I found this." He bent over and pulled something out of the pocket that ran along his shins. He waved an envelope in the air. "This was slipped under a stone three feet inside in the hedge! I saw a little speck of white sticking out. All I had to do was reach my hand in and pull it out. I waited for you to come back to open it."

When Grella arrived Tommy sat up, suddenly less exhausted. Everybody crowded around, while Tommy took the Mystery Card clue from the envelope.

"There's something else in here, too, but I'll read the card first," he said.

'You make things hard,
When you create fear,
By judging situations
Only by what you hear.
Did you ever think
Finding the hedge clue
Could be this easy?
But the Hidden Garden,
Will not be so.
These metal pieces
Will show you where to go."

Quid jumped up into the air. "So there is a Hidden Garden."

Tommy shook out the contents of the envelope and held up eight pieces of hard gray metal.

"Hmmn. Maybe they form the shape of something that's very familiar, but a little different," Quid said.

"Where could pieces of metal lead?" Tommy wondered.

"I was close, I think, when I was in the maze. I saw a marker to the hidden garden," Grella said, "but I couldn't find it and I got lost over and over. I've never been in so many circles in my life."

"Don't forget there are Deceptor clues, too. That's probably what you saw," Blake said.

Grella went on talking. "I hadn't planned to stay in the hedge. I just dove in to show you I could. I didn't like having you send me to the archives to see Filey, Tommy Smurlee!"

"Well you should have discussed it with me first. Diving into the hedge maze was dumb and dangerous, Grella. Don't ever go off by yourself like that again!" Tommy ordered. His eyes looked at her more softly than the tone of his voice showed.

"I know, I'm sorry," Grella murmured.

"Let's get some rest," Tommy said.

"I think Counselor Zeller knows where the Hidden Garden is," Blake announced.

"He brought it up today during today's session," Quid added. "I'll try to find out from him tomorrow."

The next day Quid bumped into Counselor Zeller unlocking his room. He was dressed strangely in long gray pants and shirt, a dark overcoat and black hat with a feather even though it was 85 degrees outside. Quid pushed past the other campers to get closer to him. He said, "We found more info on the Hidden Garden in the hedge maze."

Counselor Zeller gasped, opened the door to his room, and rushed past Quid.

Quid followed him into his room. Then he stopped and gawked.

All the chairs were facing the back wall. Zeller carried his notes to the rear of the room. "Who did this? There will be no Hidden Garden discussion until these chairs are back in order." He hurried out of the room.

One by one the rest of the campers arrived and talked about what happened. The campers fixed the chairs and waited a few minutes, but Zeller didn't return. They stood chatting until the session ended.

That afternoon, when the campers arrived for Part II of Zeller's session, he was wearing his black outfit and standing outside his room. The door now had five locks and chains on it. Counselor Zeller took six minutes to undo them all. He announced with a grin as he unlocked the last one, "The room will be in order today."

Quid said nothing.

When Counselor Zeller opened the door and looked into the room he gasped, "Not again." All the chairs faced sideways. Zeller screamed. "That's enough! I mean it I! I want order!"

Blake and Quid looked at each other. "Who's he talking to?"

The next day, when the campers arrived, there were no locks on the door. The campers opened it and walked in. The entire room was helter-skelter. Chairs faced every which way.

"So much for order," Tommy said.

It took ten minutes to get the session officially started because Counselor Zeller never came. He was gone. No one knew where he'd disappeared to. After five minutes Toodle went to tell Director Croggle.

The Director arrived a few minutes later. "I tried to get another counselor to come handle the session, but no one has time until next week. I regret to inform you that Counselor Zeller has been reported to be studying the occult and dabbling in witchcraft which is totally against camp rules. We also discovered strange happenings going on in his lab and in his living quarters. Zeller will stay in confinement while we investigate further. "

Blake yelled, "I knew it!"

The Director glared at him and Blake slunk in his seat. "Please tear up any material from Counselor Zeller that might make reference to these topics."

"He never said a word about spooks," Toodle said.

"How do we know what he was doing?" Grella said. "He might have been casting demonic spells on us."

"No worry, we've got angelic protection," Quid reminded her.

"Maybe you do, but I'm not sure about me," Toodle said.

"You can be sure," Grella said sweetly to Toodle.

"Well, I know I don't!" Piney said. It was hard to say if he was bragging or complaining.

"Well, you can. It's your own fault!" Grella said.

Croggle glared at her because he was still speaking. "Counselor Hintley will take over this session next week. Until then this period will be a special time to work on your camp projects or the G.U.M. (Great Unsolved Mystery.)"

"I'm going to spend my time finding the way through the mystery maze," Piney whispered.

"Is there another? You mean the hedge maze?" Tommy really couldn't be sure. Every single day he was finding something new at Dunster's.

"Why bother with that," Grella said to Piney. "If only you guys can find the Hidden Garden!" "I wonder if Zeller's the only counselor who knows about the Hidden Garden," Quid said.

"Maybe he doesn't even know for sure. If Zeller's connected with Dagta, he could be faking clues," Toodle said.

"Let's find Zeller's place of confinement and ask him," Tommy said.

"Good idea. When do we go?" Quid asked.

"We have no time to waste. Tonight."

Chapter 10
Zeller to the Cellar

That evening Tommy and Quid climbed the rickety, seldom used stairs to the fifth floor. No campers were ever invited there. The counselors' sleeping quarters and offices were on the 5th. "Some camp," Quid said, "this building is more like a medieval castle."

"I'm nervous being here," Tommy said.

"I'm scared to death. What if someone sees us?" Quid tried to keep himself from pacing up and down the hall.

"That's why we didn't use the Wind Whoosher. What do the counselors do in their offices up here?" Tommy asked.

Quid shrugged. "Personal experiments and research. They only work as counselors for two weeks. The Director lets them stay here and work on their own inventions in exchange for counseling us."

Tommy led the way along the dark, creaky corridor. "I've heard this is called the 'Creaky Corridor, wonder why," he said.

"I can't imagine," Quid whispered. Suddenly a voice bellowed, "Is everything taken care of?" in an enormously loud tone. It was so dark Tommy almost bumped into the man before he saw him.

Tommy scrunched against the wall. Quid folded himself silently behind Tommy.

The man didn't seem to sense their presence.

Tommy waited a few seconds then peered out at the dim shadow of a thin, little man.

"Who's that? I never saw him before," Tommy whispered.

"I think it's Counselor Tinns. He referees the Slap/Dash games."

They overheard Tinns saying to Zeller, "Are you sure it's well-hidden? This is an advanced bunch, you know, very inquisitive."

"We're doing regular checks."

"Can I trust that?" Tinns shook all over, not just once, several times, like the insides of a bottle of salad dressing. Then he said, "Just the thought that this could be discovered too soon upsets me."

Quid wiggled his nose and sniffled, fighting back a sneeze.

Tinns and Zeller heard the noise Quid made at the same time.

Zeller pulled Tinns into the nearest open sleeping room and shut the door. A few minutes later, Zeller peeked out.

They heard another door open and close down the hall, but it was too dark to see what room Zeller entered.

"I thought Zeller was in confinement until his case was reviewed," Quid said continuing down the hall.

"I guess he's allowed out in the Creaky Corridor and the counselors' labs," Quid said.

"I hear that Dagta prowls around up here, too. Orson's demonic power," Quid said.

"Who's there?" roared a gigantic voice next to them. Quid's body started to shiver. Tommy forced himself to look. No one appeared to be there. Then another figure darted out from a room behind them and stood in the shadows near them.

"Did that shape come out through the door?" Quid asked through shaking teeth. "Or did it pass through the wall?"

Tommy's stomach felt like it had turned upside down. "I couldn't tell who or what made that roar. It sounded like a voice from under the ocean, but coming from nowhere. That can't be," Tommy said. "At least the second shape looked like a man."

"But not like any counselor I ever saw."

The personless voice spoke again, closer now. "I need my swat gun. And get my torch." The sound seemed to come from inside Tommy's skin.

"Swat gun!" Tommy and Quid raced to the stairs and nearly toppled down. Quid caught himself on the edge of the top step.

"Stay still," Tommy ordered. "Whatever the things are, they're going the other way. Quick, we can check the rooms before they come back."

"I don't think I want to."

"C'mon, hurry. That's why we came."

They passed Counselor Spindlestick's open door. He was standing at a table pounding on a piece of metal.

Quid squinted through the keyhole at the next door.

"Who's in there?" Tommy whispered.

"Don't know, I think it's Zolten. His back is turned this way. He's shaping a life-size piece of hollow clay, big as Toodle."

"Let me see. Wow," Tommy said. "You're right. Somebody could put Toodle inside that thing."

They crept on stopping to peek though cracks in open doors and keyholes in closed doors. The dim light from Quid's penlight guided their steps as he turned it off and on.

Finally Tommy spotted Zeller again in the back of the end room sitting in a chair with his head down. His eyes appeared to be focused on a book he was reading.

They snuck in silently and shut the door behind them.

Zeller looked straight at them. The air seemed to freeze around him.

"We came to ask some questions, Counselor, about the Hidden Garden."

When Zeller saw Tommy and Quid he bumped the vase next to him. It broke into smithereens. Zeller jumped up and said, "Oh no you don't. Stay away from me."

He sped past them, out the door. They were on his heels when suddenly he disappeared.

"Zonk, gone into the air," Quid said waving his arm to make his point.

"Forget it. Zeller is never going to tell us anything! He won't even talk to us. Why is he so afraid? We better go," Tommy said.

"Zeller! Who's looking for Counselor Zeller?" the giant voice boomed. A torch moved down the hall as if held by an invisible arm.

Another minute and it would be right in their faces.

Tommy was sure his lungs stopped working.

Quid's stomach stiffened.

Quid and Tommy had no choice but to run back into Zeller's room. Tommy slammed the door and locked it.

"Remember, the shape that seemed to come through walls. Even with a locked door we're not safe," Quid said quaking.

"Quiet! Let me think. There must be another way out. We'll find it. Trust me," Tommy said. He had no idea how, but he would. "Take the bigger pieces of the broken vase, Quid."

"Why?"

"Do as I say. It may come in handy. Everything has a purpose."

Quid grabbed a plastic bag and put the remains into it.

Tommy searched the room for another exit. The windows were too high. Then he saw a square opening, a chute, in the far wall. The sign over it said "Lab Laundry."

"Quid look!"

"What is it?" He hurried over to the wall.

"A laundry chute. Get in."

"I'll never fit."

"Oh yes you will. And I'm coming in with you."

Quid's shoulders got stuck in the door. Tommy pushed with all his might and got him through. He climbed in behind Quid, reached back and pushed the button that said "Send" on the door panel. A grinding noise followed and then off they zipped.

"Whereeeeee does this go?" Quid yodeled.

Tommy prayed they wouldn't get stuck and be lost forever in the laundry chute. What a living nightmare that would be!

Suddenly they flopped out on a mountain of sheets. The fabric softened their fall.

"Where are we?" Quid asked.

"It must be the basement." Tommy said. "What a ride!"

"Want to go again? Just kidding! Nobody is going to believe us about this," Quid said.

They sneaked back to their rooms checking often to see if they were being followed.

"Don't tell anyone where we were until we can figure this out," Tommy said.

"We're no closer to the Hidden Garden than we were. And I'm not going back to the Fifth Floor ever again!" Quid sighed.

"Forget Zeller. We'll find it another way."

But before they could discover the Hidden Garden, they had another problem.

Chapter 11
The Secret Spring

"Lots of springs feed Lake Watonka. But only one is the Secret Spring, that flows into the Hidden Garden," Counselor Hintley said.

"Our mystery this year at Dunster's has a clue located at the Secret Spring," he confided. "A solemn oath must be taken by every one of you Dunster campers never to divulge the whereabouts of this spring after you locate it. If you do you must sign over your entire future inheritance to the camp."

Tommy gasped.

"You may go there only once, to collect the clue," Counselor Hintley explained. "The trick will be finding it."

Grella raised her hand. "I already know where it is, Sir."

"What's that, Grella?" Counselor Hintley was a little hard of hearing, but refused to wear a hearing aid. "Know what, my dear?"

"Where the Secret Spring is," Grella answered.

"You may think you do, but you cannot know already." He turned to the other campers. "Now you may wonder why I say that so quickly. A precise, extensive calculation is required to pinpoint the exact location of the Secret Spring. You must use your most exacting mathematical as well as intuitive skills. No fair using GPS or a computer of any kind, not even a calculator or you'll be disqualified. I will give you some guidelines, but you must think, think! Solving this problem may take several weeks. Don't be discouraged."

Grella raised her hand again. "I was out with my cat, Peetsie and found it by chance."

Clearly annoyed, Counselor Hintley said, "Approach my table, young lady. Write down on this piece of paper where you THINK the Secret Spring is."

He stood there smiling, because he was absolutely confident she'd be wrong.

Grella scratched out some words with her pencil. Then she handed him the paper. Counselor Hintley read it and turned red. He immediately pulled a lighter from his pocket, held the paper in his right hand, set it on fire, and dropped it in the empty garbage can next to his worktable.

"Grella," he said solemnly, "you are disqualified from work on this clue."

Grella's mouth dropped open. "I thought you'd be pleased."

"Go immediately to the library, Grella."

She rose slowly. "But I didn't do anything wrong!" Tears jumped into her eyes and threatened to run down her face.

Orson chuckled from his table behind her.

"You will stay in temporary isolation," the Counselor hissed, until you assure me you will never reveal this information to the other campers."

Grella's sob sounded as if she'd been sent to Siberia for life.

Tommy's eyes bulged from their sockets. He raised his hand and said in a small voice. "We won't let her tell us, sir, we promise, but don't put her in isolation."

"Another word and you'll join her Smurlee."

"Oh no," Maryna cried out. "Then what would we do."

Quid slapped his notebook shut. "One less team member for one of the hardest clues and Grella was one of our best."

As Grella shuffled past him to leave, Tommy whispered to her, "If you found it, we will."

"I didn't," Grella said, "Peetsie did. Cats are very smart."

Right after lunch the Silver Team headed for the dorm.

Tommy said, "If Peetsie led Grella there, he can lead us."

Blake pulled a pick from one of his pockets to unlock the door to Grella's dorm room. Peetsie was nowhere to be found. Her cage was gone too.

"She's an indoor cat. Where could Peetsie have gone?" Everyone looked around in amazement.

Quid came running down the hall. "Peetsie has been impounded."

Somehow they'd find the Secret Spring and the Hidden Garden without Grella or Peetsie.

Hintley had helped a bit by telling them at least that the Hidden Garden was real.

Tommy ordered everyone on his team to spend every spare minute between sessions and all free time Saturday and Sunday scouring the grounds for a Secret Spring or Hidden Garden. Everyone, that is, except Mr. Toodle and Molar. They were assigned to study the thirty-page complex math formulas Hintley had passed out to guide them to the Secret Spring.

"Gardens and springs are big," Tommy said, "I mean, you can't hide them well. We'll explore the grounds until we find them. Keep a record of everywhere you go and tonight we'll compare notes. Go in two's if you can. If you find an envelope, don't touch it, just note the location. No mystery solving is allowed on Sunday, but going for a walk in nature is fine. If we can find the Spring before completing the math without a computer we'll be way ahead of the other teams."

"Remember," Quid said, "Grella thought at first the Hidden Garden had been in the center of the hedge maze but the marker there must have been a Deceptor Clue to throw us off the trail. Beware of Deceptor clues."

"All we know," Tommy said, "based on what Counselor Hintley hinted, is that the Hidden Garden may be at the end of the Secret Spring. We'll find it," Tommy assured everyone. He wished he felt so sure himself.

Before his next session Tommy stopped by to see Peetsie in the kennel and brought her favorite toy —the rubber giraffe she liked to sleep with.

Stopping by the kennel made Tommy late for his first Twirl Lab, which turned out to be a terrible mistake.

Chapter 12
Twirl Lab

When Tommy walked into the Twirl Lab, sixteen campers were in motion at once. He had no idea what was going on.

Each camper wore headphones attached to CD players belted to their waist. Everybody moved at different speeds and in different directions. The campers' faces glowed with sweat and something else —smiles. Everybody looked happy in here except the busy counselor who was totally absorbed in sorting some music CD's while sitting at a table to the far side of the long room.

Campers twirled past Tommy, some circled around him. Quid passed him on a fast spin. Toodle whipped by, said "Hi," and spun off.

Tommy started to cross to the other side but was bumped from the rear by Maryna. She waved and kept going.

He looked at his slip for the counselor's name for this session, Counselor Moovit. Tommy headed toward the man across the room while dodging to avoid bumping into anyone else.

The tall, skinny Counselor had his head bent over a recorder. Counselor Moovit was dressed totally in green. Tommy realized he had seen him twice before in the cafeteria, always dressed in green and always drinking a chocolate milk shake.

"Excuse me, ur, Counselor, I'm sorry I'm late."

"Yes, you certainly are. Put on a portable CD player and start twirling, you've no time to waste."

Tommy hesitated. "Twirling?"

The counselor looked up, obviously annoyed. "What are you waiting for?"

"Excuse me, sir, but I don't know how to twirl. I mean the steps look complicated."

"Of course they are. No one knows what they are! They come from your brain straight to your feet. Wait! We're having a shift."

The Counselor turned toward the twirlers. "Attention campers. We are moving TWIRL LAB outdoors. Take off your headphones, turn off your CD players. Follow me. Move smartly now."

Quid saw Tommy staring at the Counselor and nudged Tommy. "Moovit always wears green and never smiles. He says it's so the distraction of his clothing colors and his personality won't interfere with our appreciation of the mystery of music."

"What does music have to do with mystery?" Tommy asked snapping a CD player to his belt.

"Haven't you ever heard a haunting melody?" Quid laughed. He thought his answer brilliant. Tommy only groaned.

The campers lined up single file on the East Field.

Counselor Moovit brought a small stool to stand on. Tommy thought that strange because Moovit was already plenty tall.

"Now fall out, be free, free. Watch me. No CD music for this twirl." Moovit jumped off the stool and started gliding as if skating across a rink. He stopped and swept his body back in a huge arc.

Tommy quickly closed his mouth, which had dropped to his chin.

"Now you, Mr. Smurlee! Feel the music, flow with the music."

Where is the music? Tommy wondered. He heard only the sound of the wind, and the rhythm of the waves pressing upon the lakeshore. He wanted to ask, but wished someone else would. He didn't want to call attention to himself again.

Moovit was at his neck as if he'd heard Tommy. "The music is all around you, Mr. Smurlee. The Sunmaker creates exquisite music in nature. Listen!" he demanded of the entire group. "Raise your arms when you hear it."

One by one arms rose and campers began to move. Some of the campers giggled. Others laughed as they began twirling.

"Stop, stop wherever you are. Keep your pose," the Counselor ordered after several minutes had passed. "I've a mini-moment lesson for you."

Grella twirled to a stop just behind Tommy. She was thrilled to be out of confinement and twirling freely, even if she had had to promise not to tell anyone where the Secret Spring was.

"The Sunmaker made the music," Counselor Moovit said, "He's in the music as well. He's everywhere you know, not just the Chapel in the Grove. Now move again. Feel Him in the music."

"The Sunmaker's music is in laughter as well! Laugh as you twirl!" Moovit ordered and then he was off for a spin. He drew near to the Hammond brothers who were doing a twosome.

Counselor Moovit tapped Blake and stopped him mid-twirl. "Absorb the music young man. Take the joy in, let the joy out. Be a filter."

Grella breathlessly got out a question. Does Grella ever not have a question? Tommy wondered. She needed to know everything and do everything perfectly too.

"Counselor Moovit," Grella asked, "isn't there ugly music to avoid too?"

"Yes. It's ugly if it makes you hurt inside when you hear it. That's Downers music. They use it to sadden you. I'll not have that here in my session. When the music is beautiful, it's his song, and the Sunmaker is there."

Counselor Moovit turned to observe the group and opened his notebook. "Put on your portable C-D players again. Switch to a classic selection, and twirl!" He said the word like he was awarding them one million dollars. "TWIRL!"

Moovit observed Orson moving across the field clumsily. "Orson, you're chugging too slowly, open your cells. Transport the melody into your blood."

"Now campers, when we move to music, which is what twirling is, we are limited. It's best when the Sunmaker gives us a zing. Think of Him!"

Moovit pressed his battery-run CD player button to "on" and resumed twirling through the grass.

Tommy started to move. Soon he was swept into it. He found he loved to twirl.

It felt like he was flying while still on the ground —like no dancing Tommy had ever seen or done. Then he noticed Orson across the lawn heading straight for him.

He watched Orson stop midway. Orson nailed Quid with his left hip after Orson spun a particularly fierce wind-up whirl.

Quid stumbled but managed to stay on his feet.

Tommy twirled fast in the opposite direction. He looked back. Orson was gaining.

Grella spun by and warned him. "Look out, Orson's charging. He's listening to music from Peter and the Wolf on his headphones. And he's the Wolf!" I swerved away just in time.

Counselor Moovit went inside to get another set of CD's and wasn't watching now.

Orson drew within five feet of Tommy. Just as Orson was almost upon him, Counselor Moovit returned and yelled, "Stop!"

Moovit had seen Orson, too. He said, "Mr. Gartini, you may assist me with the return of the CD players when we're finished. Okay campers, start again, new music, please."

Orson snorted in Tommy's direction.

"Mr. Gartini, that is not music! Apologize for sullying our ears."

"Yes, sir, sorry."

Orson glared at Tommy Smurlee and edged closer to him.

If eyes could burn, I'd be ashes, Tommy thought.

The music began again. The Twirlers were too busy twirling to pay attention to Orson who was heading straight for Tommy again. A weight of almost two hundred pounds sledge hammered Tommy's slim body. Tommy landed head first with Orson on top of him. Then swiftly, before Counselor Moovit could see, Orson punched Tommy full force several times in the stomach, then jabbed him in the back. Tommy gasped with pain. Orson jumped up and took off.

Counselor Moovit ran over and waved his arms. "Twirler down, twirler down!" he yelled.

All the music stopped. Everyone stared angrily at Tommy for stopping their twirl. By now Orson was across the room looking every bit as annoyed as everybody else.

"Get up," Moovit ordered.

"I can't," Tommy said weakly.

Tommy felt humiliated, but the truth was he couldn't move.

"Drag him off until he gets his wind back. Gently now," the Counselor ordered. "Who will help?" He looked at Orson.

Quid and Blakely came forward instantly. "We'll do it."

"We need someone stronger." Counselor Moovit looked toward Orson again.

"No, we're sure together we can manage, really, we can."

They'd already started so Counselor Moovit let them continue.

Tommy moaned to Quid, "Don't let Orson near me again."

Counselor Moovit used his cell phone to get Nurse Allwell on the line. "Bone Check, Twirling Lab, Bone Check," he squealed into the handset.

Nurse Allwell arrived within minutes, still drying her hands. She was part time nurse and part time indoor gardener. She'd been repotting geraniums when the call came in.

She'd brought her On Sight Bone X-Ray (invented by Jersell, Dunster's Camp of 1967) and ran the pocket radio-sized instrument over Tommy's body. A few minutes later she reported, "Bruised muscles and bones, but nothing's broken."

Tommy was confined to his room the rest of the day. He fumed when he sat down to check his afternoon schedule. He'd be missing Imaginary Field trip to Egypt to see the

Pyramids and to Stonehenge, England and his first Underseas Mysteries Session.

Darn you Orson.

Tommy crawled into bed, closed his eyes and tried to remember his mother's voice. It took a while, but finally he had it right —the little lift at the end of her words and the smile in her hello. He could feel the soft white comforter with red and blue checks that they snuggled under for story time every night. The billowy white bedroom drapes, airy like gauze, fluttered on the windows of his mind. Then he thought of his Dad's rougher skin, but kind, big hands that lifted him into the air and had given Tommy his first sensation of flying. He wished he were with his parents in Africa this very moment. A tear slid onto the Red Notebook he clutched in his hands.

Grella and Quid came in to check him at four.

"Want me to hang around?" Quid asked. "I'm free next hour."

"Me too," Grella said.

"That's okay. I think I'd like to be alone now," Tommy told them.

"You've been alone long enough. It's not good to be by yourself when you're hurt. You look pretty bad," Grella said in her ever-honest, matter-of-fact voice. "C'mon let's think through this metal mystery clue. The Team is supposed to meet to discuss it tonight."

"Sorry, you'll have to meet without me. I'm just bone-squeezed tired, more than I've ever been. The concrete, the tunnel, the maze, the prowling on the 5th floor. And now Orson. I never expected all this. I'll be fine in the morning."

Grella stood very still looking at him. "You sound very sad. In fact I think it's seeping into me."

"Sunmaker," Grella prayed, "bless Smurlee. He needs you, You're the only one who can comfort him now." She set her grasshopper Fletcher in his plastic cage on Tommy's night table to entertain Tommy and left.

Sleep, real deep, dreamless sleep, the kind that leaves pit marks on your face, that's what Tommy needed now. And peace forever.

But Orson Gartini had other plans for him.

Chapter 13
Spindlesticks

The next day the sky was gray and overcast even though the air was warm. Tommy felt terrible soreness in his lower back. Otherwise he was back to his cheerful self.

He checked his laptop computer to see which activities were on today. One of the benefits of Dunster's was that no two days were ever the same. His only activities were morning labs so Tommy called a Silver Team meeting for the afternoon to figure out what the eight pieces of metal meant.

They looked like some kind of silver, but were they? Blake had them analyzed the day before in Metal Shop. He'd report the results at the meeting. Piney had the metal with him right now at his extra credit Dreamology Lab. He had the idea to hold them during his dream to see if they'd inspire some ideas. Tommy thought that was a silly plan. He'd warned Piney not to lose them.

Tommy dressed as quickly as he could while moving his tender body as little as possible. This would be his first time in this Unknown Lab and he didn't want to miss it.

The Unknown Lab was called Twickles. Whatever that was.

Tommy sat down and looked up the word on his laptop computer. He read from the screen, "Twickles are wax creations with short wicks that make a twick-twick sound as they burn."

He saw a picture of the Twickle lab on his computer screen when the lab was empty of campers. It showed one main candle with a bluish glow placed on a pedestal surrounded by fifty or more unlit wax forms in intricate shapes. Shelves stretched across the back of the room where the camper's candle creations were drying.

Twickle, twickle, little candle, he hummed to himself as he headed to the lab. The door had a coating of wax that had hardened into multi-colored wax icicles. Tommy stood several minutes examining the blended colors. Never miss a chance to experience the beautiful sights around you, Mom had taught him that.

Inside Tommy saw his strangest camp session yet. There were small tables with two to four campers at each. Hundreds of candles all around the room were spitting wax as they burned.

Tommy found a chair next to Molar at a worktable.

"Sit down and get started. Your table mate will help," the Counselor bellowed from across the room not taking his hands off the warm wax he was shaping into an eagle.

Tommy raised his eyes at Molar who had been to the Twickle Lab last summer. Molar guessed Tommy's unasked question, What do I do?

Molar explained, "We're supposed to be making twickles out of wax. Draw a shape of anything you want on the computer, the more unusual the better —rhino, armadillo, hang-glider. Press the mold key and the shape will be spit out of the special printer over by the door. Then select your wax colors and fill the molds. Be sure to slip a wick down the center before the wax dries. The experienced Twicklers from previous year's camps have a quota – some as high as ten.

Spindlesticks will probably let you do five today because it's your first day. I'm doing seven."

The air in the room was 80 degrees, summer-sweaty hot. Counselor Stirl, nicknamed Spindlesticks by the campers because of his long, skinny limbs, kept the air conditioning off because he was always cold.

Today Spindlesticks wore a plaid flat cap, socks up to his knickers, and a long sweater. "Doesn't he know it's summer?" Molar commented.

Tommy kept his voice low and whispered to Molar what had happened on the fifth floor. "We heard a voice like a giant's and felt a coldness like we'd stepped into a meat freezer."

Molar stopped work and listened mesmerized. "Do you think it was Dagta talking to you?" he asked.

"I don't know. We only heard a voice and saw a shadowy figure." Tommy shuddered. "It seemed to pass through the walls."

"Dagta can be invisible you know."

Tommy saw Spindlesticks looking his way.

"I expect so," Tommy said.

"You don't think Dagta's a person like us?" Molar picked up his work again.

"Not if he's demonic."

"And evil and powerful." Molar slipped a wick into a bird shape. "He has demons he sends to work for him."

Tommy leaned back in his chair. "That explains who may have been with him."

Molar's eyes popped with curiosity.

Suddenly Counselor Spindlesticks appeared at their table and Molar busied himself putting the finishing touches on his red cardinal. "What were you saying here?" the Counselor asked.

"Oh, excuse me sir. Was I talking too loud?" Tommy asked politely.

"Excuse me, yes, I heard you."

"Sorry, Sir. I didn't know we couldn't talk in here," Tommy said.

"The question is whether this is an appropriate time for talking. Maryna, you were in here yesterday. You should know. Doesn't the creative process flow best in silence?"

Maryna raised her head from her twickle work, "Definitely. No talking during the height of imaginative thought."

"Exactly! Silence speeds the imagination." Spindlesticks towered over Tommy. "This is the last time you will be warned. Is that clear?"

"Absolutely, sir."

"And what is my work principle, Molar, tell Mr. Smurlee. He's a new camper like Maryna, and obviously doesn't know."

Maryna recited in a singsong voice, "Whether the task is great or small, do it well or not at all."

"Thank you, excellent. Campers, repeat please the work principle that applies to everything we do."

The campers chanted the words in unison and Tommy chimed in as best he could.

"Mr. Smurlee, I'll expect seven twickles from you before you leave."

Just then the timer on Spindlesticks' watch beeped. "I shall return in ten minutes to check your progress." With that he hurried out the door.

"Where's he going?" Tommy asked Molar.

"Out for a chew. Chewing gum isn't allowed in the buildings. Even so he's acting awfully strange today."

"I wonder if he heard what I said about our visit to the fifth floor," Tommy wondered aloud.

"Shh! Don't let Orson hear. He's working at the table in the rear."

Instantly Tommy felt a chill. "Orson's in here!" He rubbed his back remembering. "I prefer to keep my distance from Orson Gartini."

Tommy stood and carefully began to carry the three-dimensional star he'd made to the wick table. On the way he had to walk past Orson's table.

Orson saw him coming and slyly stuck his leg out.

Tommy didn't see it in time. He stumbled and fell. His star was smushed into a blob of wax.

The fall was bad enough. But even worse Tommy knocked over the pedestal where Spindlesticks' beloved stuffed owl, Saggykins, perched.

"Darn you Orson. I've had enough of you!" Tommy yelled.

Things would have been okay if the owl had fallen backwards, but Saggykins went straight down onto a side table containing three recently lit pillar candles. The owl turned into a blazing ball. Tommy grabbed for a cloth from the coat and apron rack to put the fire out. It happened to be Spindlesticks tan raincoat.

Better to use Spindlesticks' coat than burn down the camp. Tommy made a split second decision.

Chairs crunched and scraped as campers fled the room.

Grella ran to get Director Croggle.

Tommy stomped out the remains of the fire. The whole thing was over in less than five minutes.

When they saw that the fire was out, one by one the campers tiptoed back in to see the remains of the owl. They sat down quickly before Spindlesticks returned. Molar shivered at the thought of what would happen to Tommy. He wished Tommy would sit somewhere else.

Tommy said nothing. He was too petrified to speak. He wanted to run, too, but he was responsible for this. How could he respect himself if he ran?

Counselor Spindlesticks strolled back in and unwrapped his scarf from his neck while sniffing the air. Is something burning? On his way to the coat rack he passed the overturned pedestal. He glanced around frantically. "Where's my Saggykins, my Saggykins?"

Then Spindlesticks saw the remains of his owl. He clutched his own head as if he'd been shot. Tommy prayed he wouldn't have a stroke.

Tommy stood. "I'm sorry, sir. It was an accident."

"What have you done, Tommy Smurlee?" Spindlesticks picked up the charred piece of round metal that had held Saggykins' stomach stuffing. Then he saw a fragment of his coat. "You're sorry?!? Not half as sorry as I'm going to make you!"

Just then Grella returned with Director Croggle.

"What's going on here?" Director Croggle demanded.

"It was an accident, sir," Tommy said.

"My owl is destroyed." Spindlesticks sputtered. He lunged for Tommy's neck.

"Spindlesticks, go to your office and rest. You've had quite a shock. I'll handle this," Director Croggle said.

"First, I must see that my other animals are okay." Spindlesticks raced around the room checking the huge stuffed crow couple, Caw and Maw. His pheasants, stuffed so full they looked like their skin might pop, were fine. The moosehead was okay, the antlers on the rear wall intact. The Counselor also examined his four stuffed cats.

"Everything else checks out."

"Come with me," Director Croggle said to Tommy speaking in his sternest voice while Spindlesticks was within hearing distance. Spindlesticks gave a last hateful glare at Tommy and stomped out the door.

Tommy followed the Director toward his office. They passed Counselor Pettypoint patrolling the halls. She glared at Tommy assuming he was in trouble from the look on Director Croggle's face. Tommy's ears were burning hot, and his knees kept trying to bump each other.

Director Croggle's assistant, Viola, was at a desk in his outer office. "Viola, you may take your break early."

"Yes, sir."

Viola hunched her shoulders and hiked past Tommy all the while giving him a "Shame on you" look.

Tommy carefully avoided the chair his Grandpa had sat on. He was glad Croggle's face didn't have that mean, stern look he'd seen when they first met. But he wasn't prepared for the slight smile breaking across the Director's mouth now.

"So that you understand what's going on here, Smurlee, Spindlestick's is one of our few married counselors and his wife won't let him keep his stuffed monstrosities at home."

"Really, sir."

"Can you guess why?"

"No, sir."

"It's because they stink there. And they stink here at Dunster's, Smurlee. And now we have one less stink. You've done us a service."

"I have?"

Croggle opened his bottom desk drawer and took out a can of peach room freshener. He sprayed it around his desk and even on his suit.

"The smell travels with one, you know. Want a squirt?"

"Yes, thanks."

"Where was I? Oh yes, Spindlesticks is good with the twickles, which is why I keep him on staff. But the stink of those old stuffed relics has made the janitor threaten quitting. Oh it's not bad when all the candles are burning. Many of them are scented which helps tremendously. But you should smell the room when the candles aren't lit." Croggle squeezed his nostrils together to make his point. "Am I making myself clear?"

"Perfectly."

"Now, should you trip again, you will have only a minimal punishment. This will remain between us. But remember we can't risk actually having a massive fire."

"No sir." Tommy had no intention of destroying any more of Counselor Spindlesticks stuffed creatures.

"He'll want another dead owl to stuff, although they are protected, aren't they? Well never mind, we may be able to find one somewhere. Maybe the staff can scare up one."

Tommy was thinking of his empty bank account. He'd just bought a shipment of mice for his boa constrictor that he left with his grandparents.

" You will have to pay for a replacement coat for Spindlesticks. Have you the money for it? Or will I have to call your grandparents?" Director Croggle asked.

"No, sir, please don't. I don't want to ask them. Isn't there some work I could do here to pay?"

"Well Spindlesticks needs an assistant, but I hardly think you'll do." Croggle flipped through some papers on his desk.

"No, I suppose not."

"Let me think on it. The General Fund may be able to kick in for it. You've done us a service and all. Now I must ground you the rest of the day and evening, but that's a small price to pay for almost burning the camp down."

"Thank you, sir."

"And keep this discussion confidential. You've been dealt with to the full extent of Dunster's law if anyone asks."

"Yes, sir."

Tommy hated to miss the Silver Team meeting tonight. He called Grella from his room. "I can't be there tonight. Orson's had a go at me again, but I'm doing better now. I'm putting you in charge. Have Blake e-mail me a report later, okay?"

The report never came.

Chapter 14
Stuck in the Muck

There were no organized Sunday camp sessions so the campers took to the game fields, the beach, the woods and gardens.

The Silver Team members had decided at their meeting the night before to head out separately to hunt for the Secret Spring and Hidden Garden. Blake had been so eager to be the first started that he forgot to e-mail Tommy about their search.

Tommy had planned to go anyway. He started right after his hour-long visit to the Sunmaker in the chapel on the grounds. After that he felt better inside but after three hours of walking his feet hurt, his head ached, and he'd swallowed all the water in his water bottle. To top it off he wasn't sure which was the quickest way back. He wished he had someone with him for company. He was tired and lonely, but wouldn't quit now.

Tommy hated to admit it, but his team was stumped. The Metal lab hadn't been able to identify the substance. Piney had no dream revelation about the eight metal pieces and gave them back.

Tommy took the pieces from his pocket and sat down and played with them. There must be something we're missing. "I wonder if they're a puzzle?" He asked aloud.

Maybe if he twisted one sideways, no, he turned it upside down, there, each had one side flat. Could he make them fit together somehow? When he tried, they formed a strange shape. It reminded Tommy of something, but what? He pulled out his miniature map of Dunster's and laid the metal pieces on top of the various ponds and buildings that dotted the grounds. He placed them over the shapes of the small hexagon-shaped boathouse and other outbuildings. He tried fitting them over the shape of the big pond. Every structure was covered except a shed of some kind about six hundred yards back from the small pond in a stretch of woods.

Could the Hidden Garden be near this shed? They didn't need to find the Secret Spring first if they could find the Hidden Garden without it.

Tommy felt energy flowing back into his arms and legs. He made a few notes in the mini notebook he carried when it wasn't convenient to bring his full-size Red Notebook. Carefully he put away the map and metal pieces and headed in the direction of the shed.

This was no time to run into Orson Gartini but he did! Orson looked bigger than ever in his red teeshirt.

The minute Tommy came upon Orson he knew Orson had broken the rule about not using magic.

Orson hadn't seen him yet, but Tommy saw the long stick in Orson's hand. Then Tommy saw Quid out in the middle of a field standing with his arms tied behind his back and his legs bound.

Orson threw the stick down. Instantly the field in front of him became a giant sinkhole.

Whoosh!

Orson quickly picked up the stick.

As Tommy watched Quid was sucked down in the twelve-foot deep swimming pool-sized hole.

"Oh no you don't," Tommy yelled running up to rescue Quid. "You're not going to hurt Quid. Change that back." Orson waved his stick again and grinned.

Ploosh!

The sinkhole started filling with wet cement.

"That should keep you where I want you." Orson laughed.

"You big bully. Pick on someone your own size." Tommy threw himself at Orson with all his might. Energized by his fury, he managed to knock Orson to the ground. Then Quid started to scream. Tommy lifted himself up to see what was happening to him and Orson took to the woods.

Cold, dark rage seethed inside Tommy. "I'll deal with you later!" he yelled after Orson.

Tommy removed his socks and shirt and tied them together to make a rope. Then he approached the huge hole at stared down looking for Quid.

Tommy couldn't see him at first. "Where are you Quid?" He yelled. "Answer me!"

Then Tommy saw him at the far end of the huge hole stuck in the cement. He'd fallen over, but managed to get into a sitting position. That was all he could do with his arms and feet tied.

"Get me out!" Quid screamed. "The cement is getting deeper."

"I'm coming!"

Tommy started slipping and sliding. He thrashed his arms to try to balance. "Hang on, Quid. I'm almost there."

Not only was the cement getting deeper, it was starting to harden.

How could he drag Quid out, when he could barely move around himself? Tommy prayed, *Sunmaker, I know you hear me, you see what's happening, please help us.*

Piney wasn't planning to take the Redweb Trail back to the dorm, but he found his feet going that way.

The day was clear and the air still. From afar off he thought he heard voices. He stopped to listen. Someone was yelling, "Help." Piney started running in that direction.

He heard it again. "Help!" It sounded like Quid!

Piney increased his speed until sweating and puffing he stopped for breath. Good thing. The earth in front of him had disappeared. He couldn't believe his eyes. "What happened to the ground?" He reached the edge of the sinkhole and peered in.

He saw Tommy Smurlee stirring the concrete around Quid with his hands and sloshing his legs to keep the cement from setting around them. Tommy could barely keep himself moving, let alone pull Quid out. The cement was inching higher every minute.

Piney rubbed his eyes. Where had this big pool of cement come from?

Then Tommy happened to look up. He saw Piney and moaned, "Piney, we need help! I wanted angels."

"Well you got me! Want me to leave?"

"No! Get us out!" Quid gasped.

"Find a branch to throw us," Tommy ordered. "Don't come in or you'll be stuck too! That's what happened to me."

Piney looked around. "Wait! I'll be right back." Piney ran toward a grove of trees several yards away. When he reached the nearest oak tree he pulled on a branch. It was too small. He ran to another tree and climbed out onto a long limb. He bounced on it with the force of all his weight. When the limb started to crack, Piney jumped to the ground. He was amazed when the branch popped off.

Piney dragged the limb to the sinkhole. Slowly he pushed it across the cement keeping it on the surface.

Quid saw him. "That'll never reach!"

"No," Tommy's voice came out in a whisper. "Quid. Don't give up. Watch." The limb seemed to grow longer as Piney shoved it out.

Wet cement seeped around Tommy's waist. It had reached Quid's shoulders now.

The branch was almost within grasp.

"Grab hold and I'll drag you both across," Piney yelled.

Tommy strained forward until his fingers touched the jagged wood. With his other hand he grasped Quid's shirt at the neck and started to pull steadily.

Piney took almost twenty minutes to haul Tommy and Quid across the concrete little by little. The cement was hardening fast. Piney huffed and puffed with all his might.

"I hear a sound like thunder," Tommy said.

"It's probably Orson using magic again and coming back to check on us," Quid wailed. "Hurry up!"

Piney grunted. "Just a little farther and I'll have you out."

"I can't hold on much longer." Tommy held his head as high as he could to keep his nostrils from being filled with cement as the two were dragged across. "Quid keep your mouth shut tight."

Piney gave one more huge heave and they reached the edge of the cement sinkhole. He helped Tommy up. Together they tugged Quid out.

Piney pulled his jackknife from his pocket and sawed through the cords around Quid's arms and legs. Then he pulled on Quid's arms while Tommy shoved Quid from behind. "Get up the hill fast!"

"Run!" Piney said.

"My legs are too stiff," Quid said. "I can barely walk."

As they ran they heard a roar. Quid stopped petrified. "He's coming. Orson must have looked into the empty sinkhole."

"We've almost reached the clearing. Don't stop," Tommy yelled.

"Fear not for I am with you." Quid quoted to encourage himself. "When you walk through the fire you will not be burned."

"Only this time, run, don't walk!" Tommy said as he shoved Quid.

Quid started moving.

"Keep going until we get back to the main camp building," Tommy ordered.

They ran as fast as they could.

Orson followed them to the camp buildings then halted.

On safe territory Quid, Piney and Tommy slowed to a walk.

Grella came running out of the Dream Wing. "Well if it isn't the three musketeers." She drew closer and her eyes widened horrified. "What happened to you? Who did this?"

"We need to hose down quick!" Tommy's toes were clogged with concrete. Quid looked like a dissolving statue.

"Orson was rule breaking with magic," Quid said.

"Let's report him." Grella said squeezing her hands into fists.

"We should. Orson's a cheat!" Piney said.

"How do we prove it?" Quid asked.

"We can't," Tommy said. "Quid's okay, that's what matters. The Sunmaker saved us by sending Piney."

"Take care of yourself, guys," Grella's words held sweetness and sadness. "We almost lost you. Where are you going now?" she asked falling into step with them.

"To get clean clothes and wash. Then to read some Holy Words," Tommy said.

"I'm going for a dream and sleep," Quid said.

"Grella, have the team meet us at Crinkleton's old boathouse at 5 a. m.," Tommy said. "It should be getting light by then. I think I know the answer to the Mystery Clue of the metal pieces and where the Hidden Garden is. We'll go from the boathouse."

"Tell me and I'll let you know if you're right," Grella insisted.

"No, be at the old boathouse at 5 a.m. I don't want to get you in trouble if I'm wrong."

They staggered off sloshing toward the dorm. It took half an hour to hose down enough to walk into the building.

Tommy woke late at 4:45 after a restless sleep. Piney was already gone. Tommy dressed quickly and hurried to the boathouse. The Silver Team members were all waiting outside except for Grella.

"Where's Grella?" Piney asked.

"I don't know, but I left a note under her door," Blake said. "I only hope no one else finds it first. I have a feeling Orson's team isn't far behind us and we've lost time with the problems we've had!"

The six-sided boathouse had an old lock on the door that Blake picked easily. Inside they found several pieces of faded wicker furniture. Old newspapers and antique bottles stood in a corner. Tommy explained his hunch about the spring.

His eyes went straight to a framed map on the wall, a decrepit looking thing.

"Here's what we want," Tommy said. He pulled out his map, passed around his magnifying eyeglasses pointing out the area he'd marked H G.

"Look," Quid said, "there's a scraggly line on the map running into that area."

"Right," Tommy said. "That may be the Secret Spring." He marked the area and checked his compass. "I'd say it's about two miles from here, southwest."

Blake whistled softly. "What do you suppose would be in a Hidden Garden?"

"Who knows?" Quid said.

"We'll follow the line indicated on this map and find the Hidden Garden before they do," Tommy said. "I think I can estimate its location."

They headed off into the breaking day.

Tommy found the path indicated by the line on the map but it was extremely narrow. At times they walked sideways. Always they had to guard their faces from snapping branches.

"I'm hot," Maryna complained, "I wish Grella was here. I forgot my water bottle."

"This will help." Toodle gave her a piece of grape gum.

After about a half hour of walking Tommy said, "This should be it."

They came to a clearing.

Blake drew in his breath. "The Hidden Garden is beautiful!" he said.

Even though it was flowerless, the garden was filled with unusual plants with colored leaves. They had been planted around perfectly sculpted miniature statues. Each statue was about three-feet high and was dressed in real clothes!

Tommy read the names at the base of the statues. Ezra, Nehemiah, Zechariah, Micah. "Look they're all important men in history." A plaque at the entrance read, "That these men and their faith will not be forgotten."

"How come none of the previous campers from Dunster's seemed to know about this?" Blake asked.

"Probably because it's so new. The concrete walking stones aren't worn at all. Maybe the garden will be unveiled for the entire camp after the mystery is solved," Quid said.

"Did you notice what's different about the statues?" Tommy asked.

Quid looked again. "They're all wearing real clothes, but the fabric is almost an inch thick."

Tommy said, "That must be so the garments hold up in all kinds of weather."

Blake examined a label on the back of Nehemiah's cloak. "They're called 'Forever Creations.' I bet they never wear out."

The branches near the end of the trail began to rustle.

"Who's that?" Tommy whispered.

"Oh no, Orson's found us," Quid said. "Hide."

To their relief only Grella appeared in the clearing.

"Grella, you scared us!" Blake said relieved.

Maryna ran over and hugged her. "Look at these cute statues, Grella!"

"They're gorgeous," Grella said bending over to touch the sleeve of the garment on Ezra.

Tommy said, "Great, Grella! You're here." Tommy bent over to tie his shoelace while he talked. "Where were you at 5 a. m.? I can't believe you overslept."

Grella tugged the brim of her yellow baseball cap down hiding her eyes. "I wasn't going to come today because you wouldn't tell me where you thought the Hidden Garden was last night. I felt like you didn't trust me. Nobody keeps a secret better than me, Tommy Smurlee! I would never have told when I promised I wouldn't!"

"But you came now?"

Grella shrugged. "I decided I was hurting myself by being angry with you. And that was dumb, so here I am and it looks like you need me." She looked up. "I don't see anyone holding a clue envelope."

"We've just started to look," Blake said. "Help us."

Together they searched the ground, the trees, and under the stepping-stones.

But found nothing.

Grella sat down to think. A few minutes later she jumped up, "I have an idea. Let's check the pockets on the clothing. I'll start on this end with Jeremiah and Joel."

Toodle found an envelope folded up in Daniel's robe. On the outside of the envelope was a quote from the book of Daniel Chapter 10, Verse 19. "Read it Tommy."

"Don't be afraid, for you are deeply loved by God. Be at peace; take heart and be strong!"

Here is your clue:

"Where is your love?

Find the love that lasts

And the greatest of treasures

Will be yours forever.

And the next Mystery Card Clue.

"What does that mean?" Blake muttered reading it over.

"We'll have to figure it out later. If we don't get moving fast, we'll be late for our morning sessions."

"Not a word about this," Tommy said.

"If Orson knows we're this far ahead of his team, there's no telling what he'll do," Blake said.

Tommy shuddered.

Chapter 15
Medieval Battle

Counselor Artur walked in to the large activity room with two ferrets, one draped on his right shoulder, one on his left.

"Welcome to Medieval Times," Counselor Artur said with a flourish of his arm."

Tommy stared at the furry weasel-like animals with their pointy snouts and beady eyes.

Counselor Artur didn't mention the ferrets at first, but let them down to creep away. He sat down at a chair shaped like a throne. Three cats behind the Counselor stretched and hopped off their perch on a sofa to prowl nervously.

The Counselor looked out at his campers. "Who wants to hold Amelda, one of our pet ferrets, today?"

Tommy slunk in his seat on one of the old maroon velvet couches reserved for campers. He didn't like the looks of ferrets. "Too slithery, thank you," he whispered to Blake. "I'll take a cat," Tommy added.

He bent over and picked up a big Tom cat. It screeched and scratched a slivery slash along Tommy's wrist.

Tommy bit his lip to swallow to keep from yelling.

For the next twenty minutes Counselor Artur read stories about Sir Gawain. Scenes of knights jousting flashed on the huge curtain covering the wall behind Artur.

Next Artur announced: "We'll now act out parts of The 1000 Knights. Quickly get dressed in your armor please. Realism is important."

"How long do we have?" Tommy asked. He pulled on the realistic looking suit of black plastic armor.

"This session lasts all morning." Counselor Artur grinned and yelled, "Knights! Action" as he pulled back the curtain a forest scene with artificial trees and four mechanical horses came into view.

"Quid, Tommy you'll go first."

Tommy pounced on one of the mechanized horses, actually a big body bag with four legs stuffed with hard pillows. He looked around wondering what to do next.

Quid lifted himself onto another horse. He rode straight at Tommy. Each carried a jousting weapon. They jousted back and forth twice.

Tommy turned his horse too fast and almost fell off.

Quid caught him unaware and slammed Tommy to the ground. Quid fell on top of him.

He pulled a polystyrene knife from a sheath at his belt and plunged it into Tommy's chest. The blow broke the knife in two. A break was considered as good as a thrust.

"Got you!" Quid remounted quickly.

Tommy jumped back on his heavily armored artificial horse. He kicked the stirrups to begin his charge, praying he wouldn't really hurt his friend.

Counselor Artur yelled, "Feel it, Smurlee. Live it, sense it, be it. Your part is you! You are your part! You're a knight."

Tommy charged into Quid knocking Quid off his mechanized horse. Tommy stabbed him with a strong sword thrust.

Abruptly the lights flashed on. Everyone froze.

"Silence for a count of five!" Counselor Artur ordered. "Okay, Q &Q. Replace your equipment, journal this event in one paragraph, then sit on one of the couches with your recorders ready."

Tommy and the rest of the campers knew Q & Q, the code for quickly and quietly.

Minutes later they were all on their couches. The lights flashed off. Tommy, Quid and the rest of the Dunnies found themselves in total darkness.

Counselor Artur's voice pierced the air. "Record any sounds you hear for Dreamology Lab work. Tommy heard a bleep, bleep and immediately taped it on the tape recorder for future dream inspiration.

Tommy whispered to Quid, "Sorry about the last charge."

Quid didn't answer.

"I said I'm sorry," Tommy repeated.

"I'm not talking to you!"

"What's your problem?"

"That thrust was harder than it needed to be!"

"You rushed forward at the same time I thrust, I couldn't help it!"

Still no sound.

"We ought to work together."

Silence.

"The Counselor is heading this way."

When the session was over Quid bolted out the door before Tommy could reach him.

Quid's mad. Tommy felt terrible.

Chapter 16
Hanging Bird Walk

"Silver Team, be on the Hanging Bird Walk in ten minutes for the Eye-Straight session!" The announcement sounded over the loudspeaker after lunch.

Tommy knew exactly where to go. Piney had clued him in that morning when the session showed on his daily computer printout. He hurried to the concrete walk jutting twenty feet into the air from the third floor exit door. A narrow extension, only six feet wide, it had been made years ago for closer bird watching. Now the camp used it for outdoor sessions.

The swimming instructor, a twenty-one year old woman with the muscles of a gymnast, called the group to order.

"What's invisible is essential, and can often be identified, like the people skills I'm about to teach you," Counselor Kutilda said.

And the Sunmaker is invisible, Tommy thought, *I don't know how I'd get along without Him.* Tommy snapped his fingers. Of course! The answer to the recent clue was the easiest one of all. The Sunmaker was the source of love. Knowing Him was the great treasure that lasted forever. The next mystery card clue must be in the Chapel in the Woods.

"Awesome Sunmaker!" he said aloud.

"Stop it, Mr. Smurlee, no holy talk. Dagta might overhear," Counselor Kutilda said nervously.

Tommy didn't ask why out loud but his eyebrows shot up.

"Don't you know?" Grella whispered. "She thinks it might make Dagta angry."

Grella looked at Kutilda. "You're not afraid of him, are you, Counselor?" she asked aloud.

"Of course not. I could care less, I just do my job," the Counselor said shivering, "but I hear rumors of strange things."

Grella said, "I think perhaps you are scared, Counselor Kutilda. Don't you know the Sunmaker can protect you?"

"Stop talking about him. I wouldn't want anything bad to happen to urr, you," Counselor Kutilda warned.

"Thanks, but I can't stop talking about the Sunmaker," Grella said. Counselor Kutilda hushed her again.

"Not in this session, I tell you! As you may know, campers, we end our six weeks with a program where we award ribbons. Would you like an 'F' Brown Ribbon for Floop? Or do you want an 'A' Blue Ribbon for At-a-way? Or a plain old 'D' Yellow Ribbon for Doofus?"

"I'm looking for an 'A' Blue Ribbon for At-a-way, Counselor Kutilda," Grella said smiling.

"Then pay attention," Kutilda insisted. "Let's get on with our activity" She began to speak on the power of Eye-Straight. "You may be asking, 'What's that?' No, you're probably not asking, but I'll tell you anyway. Eye-Straight is looking someone in the eye when you're speaking. It creates an invisible string, a powerful, strong connection that connects you to another person."

Quid slipped onto the narrow walkway. He came late because he'd been running on the Slap/Dash field. Running ahead of time helped him stay still through the less active sessions. Lucky for him Counselor Kutilda didn't notice. She was busy using Eye-Straight with Grella.

"Now to our next topic. How do we show our interest in other people? Toodle, you may answer."

"Thank you, Counselor Kutilda," Toodle said looking pleased to be singled out. "We ask questions about their interests instead of talking about ourselves all the time."

"Excellent."

This was Toodle's favorite session, probably because he was a star at it. He liked Counselor Kutilda's ideas. Anything to do with people and manners delighted him.

He raised his hand. "Also to show interest, we can lean forward when others speak, we sit up straight to look alert, and we stand tall."

"Thank you for adding that, Toodle." Kutilda said.

Orson snickered. "Yeah, tall Toodle! That makes a lot of sense coming from you, shortie!"

The Counselor glared at Orson. So much for a string of powerful eye contact.

Orson wasn't afraid of her so he glared back. Kutilda's face turned red. She'd had her fill of Orson, but she didn't want to deal with Dagta and she'd heard Orson and Dagta were connected.

"That's all. Campers, you're dismissed."

Try as she might, Counselor Kutilda found being a camp counselor exhausting. But Dunster's paid well, and she only had to be here two weeks. Her grandparents had been trapeze artists and had taught her their skill. If only she'd joined the traveling circus when she had the chance. Maybe it wasn't too late to go.

Chapter 17
SMAC Attack

Tommy dreaded the next activity. It was his turn to take the middle in SMAC's Attack session. He'd seen what happened to campers in the SMAC Attack yesterday. *Keep thinking about the Slap/Dash coming later. You can get through this,* he told himself.

Counselor Stu Machoney, wearing gray shorts and a gray tee shirt, was waiting at the door. He didn't say hello or smile. In fact his eyes, behind dark, round eyeglasses, stared straight ahead.

The campers called Counselor Machoney "SMAC" for short because it went well with his activity.

Tommy slunk into a chair.

Quid, wiggled past the Counselor, avoiding his eyes. He whispered to Tommy, "You and I are on for today. Why doesn't the floor open up when you need it?"

"How about a tornado?" Tommy suggested.

"I'll take it."

Tommy was glad that Quid didn't seem mad at him anymore. Sharing their dread of this SMAC experience may have helped him get over it.

Grella overheard their conversation and said, "What's so tough, guys? These are only words that SMAC you."

"Yeah, sure," Tommy said unconvinced. "Have you ever been in the middle, Grella?"

"Not yet, but I'm not afraid."

"I am," Quid said. "I was in last year. Talk to us after you've been there."

"Time to get started," SMAC announced. "Smurlee, stand in the center of the room. Form a large circle around him, campers. Step smartly now, we've a large group."

When the campers had positioned themselves around Tommy, Counselor SMAC passed around a basket filled with slips of paper on which insults were written. "Everyone pick at least seven. Don't look at them yet. You may make up your own sentences also if you wish. I expect you all to participate."

Tommy looked around at the forty campers. No one would meet his eyes. He took a deep breath. Orson was missing. That was good. Maybe this was his lucky day after all.

"When I say 'Now,' Counselor SMAC ordered, "start throwing insults at Camper Smurlee."

The campers moved closer. "Now!"

"You idiot!" Maryna called out.

"You're the meanest camper at Dunster's," Molar said.

Tommy raised his hand. "Counselor, wait, these guys are supposed to be my friends. Couldn't you have the kids I don't know well attack?"

"No, it hurts more this way. Now don't interrupt again or I'll extend your time in the center." The Counselor turned his back on Tommy.

The insults resumed.

"Smurlee, put up your defense," SMAC suggested.

"What am I supposed to do?" Tommy had never been through anything like this.

"Stand tall, breathe deeply, loosen your jaw, and relax your tongue. Simple? No, but do it." SMAC ordered.

The counselor sounded like he was truly trying to be helpful, but then he turned to the circle of campers and ordered, "Blake, throw him way off balance with some really mean words."

Blake hated to do it. He read aloud the words on his attack slips. Even Blake was surprised at how easily and how well he cut down his friend.

"More." Maryna egged Blake on.

Tommy wore a Hurt-o-meter strapped to his wrist like a watch to measure his level of hurt. A screen in front of the room flashed the numbers lighting up on Tommy's wristband.

After several minutes Tommy's brain felt ready to burst. His face became hot. Who said boys didn't like to cry? A good cry would feel great, but he wouldn't do it here.

"Fire off your sensory protection signals, Smurlee."

"How do I do that, sir?"

"Remember, think calm, wherever you are, whatever is happening."

Tommy tried, he really did, but just then he saw Orson come in. Fear shot through him. Not just of Orson. The unknown. *What would Orson say? Could Tommy handle it?* That was his greatest worry. His Hurt-o-meter soared.

The Counselor noticed the reading on the screen behind Tommy immediately. "Mr. Smurlee, do you want out? Is this too rough for you?"

"No!"

Grella read the insults from her papers with tears in her eyes while holding up three fingers —the Sunmaker signal. Don't forget. Through the Sunmaker you can do all things.

Tommy sucked in air. I can make it, he told himself. Find your love source. Think of the Sunmaker quick! Still Tommy grimaced, but the meter dropped 3 degrees.

"Look out!" Grella yelled.

Orson had reached the counselor. He handed SMAC a pass. "Sorry I'm late. I had to finish my lab experiment. I hope I didn't miss anything much."

"We're working Smurlee over. Take some slips from the basket to attack him, but go easy, he's tottering."

Orson wasted no time. "You loser, what a bum! You're nothing but a puny little kid! How did you ever get into Dunster's Camp? Probably your grandparents sent you here because they didn't want you around so much this summer, that's why. Ever wonder why your parents take off on you?" Orson never even looked at the slips he'd pulled from the basket. He made up his own. Orson fired off the ugliest insults Tommy had ever heard.

These words aren't true, Tommy told himself. Still the meter swayed dangerously to the right. It took all Tommy's strength to hang on as the barrage of attacks continued.

Grella started to cry. She was penalized as an attacker and lost three points from her score.

Stand tall, tap into your peace source, Tommy commanded his body.

"It's worse when your own friends turn on you. That's the hardest attack," SMAC explained. "Keep it up, campers! The Hurt-o-meter is jumping!"

Counselor SMAC kept watch over every attacker. According to the rules no one could help Tommy.

Words, only words, Tommy reminded himself. But they felt like spears stabbing his flesh.

Then Orson swore at Tommy.

"Automatic five point loss on your score, no swearing allowed," Counselor SMAC said. "Lose ten points and you're out of the round."

Orson almost choked to keep from swearing again. He didn't want to be tossed out. Nothing would keep him from slashing Smurlee any way he could.

There were no rules for how close to the SMAC victim the attackers could get. Orson squeezed his hands into fists and put his face inches from Tommy's nose. Orson's garlic breath was as strong as his words. There was such meanness in his verbal stabs that the other attackers let him take over.

Curses under control, Orson used every other ugly word he could think of, and invented some new ones, too. "Hear it from me kid, you're a nothing. You've never been anything, and never will be. I don't care what anyone says."

Tommy's head dropped on his chest.

Orson took a step to go after Tommy and yank his head up, but Counselor SMAC put an arm in front of him. Orson muttered under his breath and spouted some more ugly words to Tommy.

"Nobody around here likes you. They're all just kissing up to you because they think you can help solve the mystery, that's all they want you for. And that's never gonna happen, see."

Orson stomped his foot down so hard that SMAC raised a yellow stick, which meant, "one more violation and you're disqualified."

Tommy felt like a piece of smushed cheese. He'd rather be stuck forever in the middle of the cement pond than stand here another minute.

"Wait until you're in the middle, you're nothing but a beast, Orson Gartini," Grella sobbed.

If anyone but Grella had said that, Orson would have turned over every table in the room to attack. They'd be his enemy forever. He glued his arms to his sides to keep from lashing out.

"No insults for anyone outside the inner circle, Grella, minus another two points," SMAC said.

122

Finally a buzzer sounded. Mercifully Tommy heard it. He silently thanked the Sunmaker and staggered out of the circle.

Counselor SMAC grabbed him by the shoulder and headed him toward the washroom. "You made it, Smurlee! First time, too, quite an achievement my boy! Quid, your turn, let's not waste time."

Tommy thought he'd be sick. He splashed cold water on his face for several minutes before he could lift his head.

Counselor SMAC popped back in after he got Quid's attack started. "Take a rest. Fine job, Smurlee. That's the worst I've ever seen anyone take an attack on a first round. How did it feel?"

"A beating would have felt better."

"Yes, yes, but you're stronger now. There will always be mean people and hard situations in life. You must learn to hang tough. Remember, with the Sunmaker's help you can get through put-downs, even persecution. You've just done it!" He patted Tommy on the back very gently. "A few more rounds and you'll be unflappable."

"I have to go back in?" Tommy started to sway.

"No, no, next summer if you come back. You passed, Smurlee. Stay here in Recovery until the activity is over. Listen to what Quid's taking in there. Magnificent!" Counselor SMAC waved his hand and was off.

Tommy's brain felt like mush. If he didn't recover soon, there'd be no more work on the mystery today. Maybe a game of Slap/Dash would help restore him.

Chapter 18
Slap/Dash

Tommy snapped back partially from his SMAC attack by the end of the day. At least he got over the worst of it, some pain would linger he figured. He was glad a competitive game of Slap/Dash was scheduled.

The smell of summer blossoms was everywhere and the crisp wind against his skin started to revive him.

He only wished he knew how to play Slap/Dash. He and Quid reached the field before the other players although the coaches had arrived.

"Welcome to the Tortor team, Smurlee," the coach said. "Since you're a new camper, Quid will go over the basics with you."

Quid walked Tommy to the end of the field. "Unfortunately we're playing the Gigs, my least favorite opponent, you can guess why."

"Gartini's a Gig." Tommy gulped, still smarting from his SMAC attack.

"Okay, let's get this instruction over with. In the Slap/Dash game instead of goals each team scores popples," Quid explained to Tommy.

"You swing the Slap stick and slap at a popple the size of a flat softball. Give it a big, full slap when you need to send the popple far and adjust to a shorter stroke when the popple target is close. The popple basket is suspended on a constantly moving pulley that runs across the field," Quid said.

"That sounds easy enough," Tommy said.

"Oh, but wait, that's just the Slap part of the game." Quid whipped his slapper stick back and forth. "You can't score with a slap into the basket. No, sir. This game is a variation of hockey and football."

"What's the Dash part then?" Tommy opened his Red Notebook to write down the instructions. One by one, the other players began to arrive.

"Two players on your team must dash past the basket line one on each side before the popple pounces out. They're called dashers. Guards will try to tackle them to stop them. There's a Pop Mechanism in the basket that causes it to come out after five seconds."

"Kind of like what I saw at the entrance to Dunster's?"

"Same principle, same inventor. The Pop Mechanism is his first successful invention —an automatic ejector."

"I knew I recognized it." Tommy made another note in his book.

"Each team Slap/Dashes for points at the same time. No guard from the other team is allowed to interfere with the slapper, but the guards can block the dashers. If the guards go after the opponents they leave their basket unguarded."

"How do you know whether it's better to guard your own basket or go on the offensive against the other team?"

"You must think quick, just like in life."

Tommy looked over at the Gigs and Tortors fidgeting on two long wooden benches. They were divided by a rivalry so intense the air between them almost smoked.

Tommy took a deep breath. This game didn't sound easy at all. He wanted to make sure he had all the numbers straight. "How many are on the field at one time?"

"Ten people total at any one time —five per team. Each team has one slapper, two dashers, and two guards. And two refs called judges."

"Sounds tough!"

"You better believe it! It's a game of skill and quick reflexes. Ah, but the hardest part of all is that the baskets are on a pulley and they keep moving farther out, so the Slap/Dashes keep getting harder. There are fourteen rounds and the game moves very fast.

"Watch. It's about to start. See the line judge out there. He's throwing the switch to start the baskets moving."

The first plays ran smoothly, but no one scored.

Orson was the next Slapper. He took his stick and slapped with all his force, but not at the basket at all, the popple went flying straight at Blake. It narrowly missed his head.

Judge Dor stalked over to Orson and yelled, "One more stunt like that and you're out of the game."

"We want a new Slapper!" The Tortor team yelled

"We're going to cream you." The Gig gallery chanted.

After the next round the first Judge Dor left the field. He was replaced by Orson's buddy, Judge Niggle.

Tommy was up as a dasher. He raced across the field and almost reached the goal for a popple point. Orson was winding up for a Slap, saw Tommy and aimed at him instead.

Orson hit his mark.

The popple hit Tommy in the back of his left leg and sent him sprawling just before the popple popped out.

The judge eyed Orson suspiciously but had to discount Tommy's dash because he wasn't on his feet when the popple pounced out.

Orson ran over to him. "What a terrible accident." Orson said to the judge, "I'm real sorry about that judge. I just missed. My aim is off today. I must need glasses."

Orson missed the next two slaps.

Then it was Tommy's turn to slap. He said, "Watch me, Quid, I'm going to make it. We need this point." Before he slapped he took a few moments to visualize the popple going into the basket.

Tommy wound up and the runners got into position. He slapped with all his might, using a rainbow arc. The popple dropped in. Both runners were almost breathless but one had gone the distance to score a point for the Tortors.

Judge Dor announced, "The Tortors win." The rest of the Tortor players came running onto the field and embraced Tommy.

Orson stalked off the field.

"He's not going to take this loss well," Tommy predicted. We better warn Grella and the rest of the Silver Team to be on the alert."

Chapter 19
Quid

Quid, Piney and Tommy met outside Grella's Imagino activity room where she was releasing her brainpower through creative movement.

Quid told Tommy and Piney, "You go in and warn her. I'll wait outside and watch for Orson."

Tommy and Piney stared through the glass rectangle on the door into the Imagino room.

They heard the counselor say, "Now do the popcorn, campers. Come, come, Grella, more pop. After eight counts become bumble bees. Buzz with more zzzzzz, Toodle."

"I'm getting tired," Grella called out.

"Don't stop yet. You're doing great!"

The music, a soft swing melody picked up. "Ready for a side-to-side caterpillar slither, arms up. Watch me," the counselor said. "Now do your own version."

"What's different about this activity from the Twirl Lab?" Tommy asked when Grella came out for a water break.

"We don't just do steps, we become things! Silly, can't you tell? Watch me now. I'm a cat." Grella crouched in the hall and began to creep around, then she jumped into the air. "Meowww."

"If you say so, Grella, only you don't look too catty to me. When will you be through?" Tommy asked. ""I think I know where to find the next clue. We're going there now, but we came to warn you to watch out. Orson will do anything to stop us. He's angry because he's behind in clues and he lost at Slap/Dash too. Blake overheard Orson telling one of his buddies that he's going after Quid again. He doesn't like Quid because he's so fast."

"He hates Quid's quotes, too, but I like them," Grella said. "I can't leave but I can come say 'hi' To Quid quick. This is practice for tomorrow's camp program. I have to turn in my videotape of these movements.

"I didn't see anyone with a camcorder," Tommy said.

"Tommy, when will you learn to respect the creative ability of Dunnies? I'm wearing one in my necklace. It shoots a projection out, then twists around and captures me from ten feet away. It's the only truly effective self-cam that's ever been made. Tutellor, Dunster's Camp of 98."

They stepped out onto the concrete wrap-a-around porch that crossed the front of the main building.

"I thought you said Quid was out here," Grella said. "Where is he?"

Tommy looked annoyed. "We left him out here. Where could he have gone! I told him to wait."

"Here's his bandanna in the grass," Piney said.

"That's strange, maybe he left it behind to alert us," Tommy said.

They looked at each other. No one wanted to speak the thought that Orson had looked very angry.

Piney said, "I bet Quid's being fricasseed, roasted, and toasted. We won't recognize him after what he's going through."

"''Don't even think like this. I'm sure he's fine," Grella said.

"Then why isn't he waiting? Let me call his room. Maybe he had to go back for something." Tommy reached into his pants pocket. "Wait, I've no phone. I must have left it in my room. Tommy was upset with himself. Where is Blake and his incredible pockets when we need him?" "Do you have your phone, Grella?"

She whipped it out. There was no answer in Quid's dorm room.

"I can't stay out here," Grella said. "I'm going back in. Fetch me when you find him."

"Counselor Doolicky may have seen him pass," Piney said to Tommy. "Remember he was going down the steps when we came."

Old Counselor Doolicky was one of the first counselors at Dunster's when the camp began. He wasn't as sharp as he used to be so he didn't work with campers anymore, but he was a whiz in the greenhouse with herbs.

"Let's find Doolicky and ask him," Tommy said.

"Right! This could be serious," Piney added.

Counselor Doolicky was in his greenhouse shredding dried dandelions and milk thistle. He liked making mysterious concoctions from the herbs he grew.

Doolicky was able to help more than they could hope for. "I saw two boys dragging Quid off. I thought they were assisting him because he'd fallen and gotten hurt. He was covered with dirt."

"Did you see which way they went?"

"No, but I heard them say, let's take him to the North woods for a dip in the lake to clean him up."

"Omigosh. Quid can't swim," Piney said.

"Shall I come and help?" Counselor Doolicky offered.

"We can handle it, sir," Tommy said.

"Good, I'm rather involved here. Let me know how things go. If he needs a bit of a pick-me-up when you find him, bring him here. I've some tasty pickle quick-lift juice that's just finished fermenting."

"We may do that."

Blake came around the corner.

"Blake, Quid's in trouble," Tommy said. "Come with us to the North woods to look for him."

"What happened?"

"We think he's been kidnapped," Piney said.

"Why are we standing here, let's go! This is my brother you're talking about!"

"Shouldn't we notify the Director first?" Tommy asked.

"No, the rules say anyone may leave the camp center for twenty-four hours to investigate a clue as long as they stay on camp property. "And maybe Quid did!" Piney offered hopefully. "Doolicky could be mistaken. Quid may have wandered off."

"Without telling us? I find that very unlikely," Tommy said. "Something terrible must have happened to him. We've got to find him fast."

Chapter 20
The Sunmaker

By nightfall Tommy and Piney had searched for hours. Quid still hadn't been found.

"Let's head to the Chapel. I want to ask the Sunmaker about Quid plus I think our next Mystery Clue is there. We can pick it up at the same time."

"Why would it be there?"

"Think, Piney. Who else is the source of love?"

"Beats me, but if you say so, fine. I'll go anywhere for a clue!"

Piney and Tommy tugged on the heavy oak door of the Chapel in the Woods and stuck their heads into a dazzling light.

Piney blinked several times before he could see anything. "I can't believe I'm here. This is my third year at camp and I've never been in this place before."

"Why not? Didn't you know about the Sunmaker's Chapel?"

"I've seen it on the map, that's all."

"Weren't you interested in investigating for yourself?"

"Not really. I'm turned off by this kind of stuff. Where's the Sunmaker anyway? The Chapel is empty."

"It only seems that way. He knows we're here. Piney, I want to ask you a personal question before I take you to the inner room."

"Sure, but maybe I won't answer."

Tommy knew someone could have general knowledge about the Sunmaker yet still not know him personally. "Piney, the Sunmaker wants only good for each of us and can turn even hard things that happen into good. Why wouldn't you love Him and want His love? I mean, what's to not like?"

"Others have said they loved me and wanted to do nice things and never did. Like my Dad for one. He was always too busy."

"But only the Sunmaker has the power to never fail you," Tommy said. "The Sunmaker never leaves a need unfilled. Trouble is most people fill the hole themselves with self-pity and grumbling or stuff and never get to see what the Sunmaker will do to help them."

"Why's that?"

"For your reason. Because they're afraid or unwilling to trust Him and depend on Him."

"Yeah? How do you know all this?"

"I've tested it Piney, I've watched the Sunmaker at work."

"You knew the Sunmaker before you came here?"

"I know the Maker of all people and things who cares for us more than we can imagine."

The rays of light in the old chapel began to vibrate.

Piney's voice was low and gruff. "I've heard enough talk."

"Okay, but as long as we're here, let's pray for Quid and ask the Sunmaker about him."

"I still don't see anyone."

"Ask the Sunmaker to give you spiritual eyes. Don't be scared. You'll get an idea of his splendor," Tommy said.

With that he dropped to the floor on his knees and removed his cap.

They heard the sound of an ocean roaring and then the back wall of the chapel was covered with a rainbow encircling a throne. From the throne came flashes of lightning. Before the throne, seven lamps were blazing. Before the throne what looked like a sea of glass glimmered. In the center, around the throne, were four living creatures like no animals they'd ever seen. Stones, rubies, pearls, diamonds, sparkled brilliantly reflecting the rays of light from the Sunmaker's veiled form.

"This description was given in the Holy Words of Revelation!" Tommy whispered to Piney.

"Omigosh!" was all Piney could say.

Tommy knelt and prayed aloud about Quid's disappearance. He told about their mystery work. He asked the Sunmaker to show them where to find Quid and then to direct them to the next clue.

Piney stood over Tommy. "What's going on? Are you getting an answer?"

"Shh. Yes, I am."

"I don't hear anything."

"It's coming in my heart. The Sunmaker is saying, 'Don't worry, Quid will be alright. You'll find him, but not immediately. Quid is becoming stronger by enduring this difficult time. You, too, must store up the truths I teach you to grow strong. Now you are learning patience and trust.'"

"Sunmaker, what about Orson?" Piney blurted out the question. It was the first that he'd spoken directly to the Sunmaker. "I mean we don't know what to do with him. He goes after us every time we turn around. He's trying to block us from solving the mystery." Piney clenched his fists. "I think there's enough of us. If we gang up and attack, we could hurt him pretty bad."

Tommy flinched. He knew the Sunmaker wouldn't like hearing Piney say that.

The Sunmaker said to Tommy's heart. "Piney can't hear Me because he doesn't really believe in Me. Tell him for Me, 'I understand your angry feelings, Piney, but don't act on them. You can protect yourself, but don't attack Orson. That would make you as bad as him. Let Me handle your battles. Sometimes you must simply wait, but only for a time.' Tell Piney for Me please, Tommy."

Tommy repeated the message to Piney who didn't say another word. He stood perfectly still listening.

Finally Tommy said, "We have to go now, Sunmaker, but we'll come again."

As they turned to go Piney saw the table near the door. It had a cardboard sign that read DGUM in violet letters and eight boxes the size of butter boxes stacked up.

"What does that mean?" Piney asked.

"DGUM? Hmmmm. I know, Dunster's Great Unsolved Mystery. DGUM. This box has to have our next Mystery Card clue. I thought so! I told you it would be here." Normally Tommy would have been thrilled with another clue. At the moment he was too worried about Quid to be super excited. Tommy took a box, determined not to open it until Quid was found.

He stopped at the door and turned back for one last look. "Mighty Sunmaker of all things. You alone are worthy of praise." Then he hurried out, with Piney behind him. Neither of them said another word about their visit to the Sunmaker.

Tommy and Piney searched some more without luck. He had a horrible feeling when he went to bed. Quid's absence bothered him so much he couldn't sleep. Tommy turned over and over. It didn't help that he heard Piney coughing in the next bed.

Tommy got up for a glass of water and tripped on Piney's arm that had rolled off his bed onto the floor. Tommy thought sure Piney would awake, but Piney pulled his arm up, punched the pillow closer to his nose and grunted.

Piney coughed again and lifted his head. "Tommy, are you awake?" he asked groggily.

"Yes."

"I feel like something horrible happened to Quid." Piney's voice was a whisper. "I wish I'd let him pace in our room without getting upset with him."

"I'm worried, too. But we're not going to find Quid in the middle of the night. We'll start looking again at daybreak." They tried to console each other.

Suddenly there was a step in the hall and a note slid under their door.

Tommy hopped out of bed and raced into the hall. No one was in sight. He ran back, grabbed the note and opened it.

He read aloud. "Come to the grove next to the North woods if you want to see Quid again. Come alone."

"Who sent it?" Piney asked.

"There's no signature."

"This is scary." Piney pulled his sheets around his chin with two fists.

Tommy said, "Get out of bed. We have to go."

Very quietly the two boys groped their way into their clothes and left the dorm.

Outside the night sky held a moon with a grayish mist surrounding it.

"Orson's waiting for us out here somewhere, I just feel it. Dagta, too, I bet," Piney said.

"Stop trying to scare us," Tommy said. They'd walked about half a mile along the edge of the woods when a voice stopped them in their tracks.

"Hey Smurlee. Is that you? I said to come alone."

136

Tommy felt a chill go through him. A boy —or was it a man – almost two hundred plus pounds of him stood right on the path in front of Tommy. He saw no way around. Migtwee, a huge cat the size of two volleyballs, peered at them from a perch on Orson's shoulder.

Piney rushed up behind him. "What have you done to Quid? Orson, did you kidnap him?"

Orson jeered, "Is someone talking to us?" Migtwee jumped down and arched his back.

"Where is he?" Tommy demanded.

"He's just ahead a few yards. We had fun playing a game with him."

"Yeah, in the middle of the night," Piney muttered.

Tommy moved past Orson with his jaw quivering. Orson let them pass, but followed.

Tommy breathed out and started running at an even pace. He saw Quid flat on the ground ahead.

"What have you done to him?" Tommy yelled at Orson.

"Now what could have happened! I better check him over with you," Orson said.

"Looks like he's passed out," Piney said. Tommy bent over to examine Quid. A bruise the size of a pin pong ball dotted his forehead. Next to him a stone lay on the grass.

Tommy gently slapped Quid's cheeks to revive him.

Quid came to and said groggily, "Where am I?" He tried to stand, but couldn't.

Tommy put a hand gently on Quid's shoulder saying, "Rest."

Migtwee, Orson's scraggly black cat, hopped back up to his perch on Orson's shoulder.

Orson the Mean Machine wasn't a boy, Tommy decided, but a huge piece of moving granite empowered by pure evil.

"Let's just say I wanted Quid to get the lay of the land, right, fricklepuss?" Orson laughed.

"Who are you calling fricklepuss?" Tommy's knees were shaking, but he got the words out.

"Stay out of my way, or I'll use my slingshot on you, too," Orson said. "You're a loser, Smurlee. Keep in mind that I always win and you'll get on fine. You're two clues ahead of us and I want you to slow down. If you don't, next time Quid might not wake up and you and the rest of your team can join him on the ground. None of you will be getting up again. This is your last warning."

A dozen blackbirds flew by with a clatter of cawing heading toward the lake.

When they passed, Orson and Migtwee were gone!

"What happened?" Quid asked.

Tommy shook his head with amazement. "How could someone that big disappear quickly and completely?"

"Dagta! I'm sure he's working with Dagta," Piney said.

"I need a good dream to clear my head," Quid said.

"And some sleep," Tommy added. "We'll help you back. We got another clue from the Sunmaker, but we didn't want to open it without you. We'll gather the team in the morning. We're going full force ahead to the next clue. Orson's threats aren't going to stop us."

Tommy refused to think about what Orson might do next.

Chapter 21
The Blue Clue

"Shake me and you will hold,
The secret to the Blue Clue
It's sweet, neat, and upbeat,
You can follow it with your feet.
Hide this box with care
After you retrieve the clue
That leads you there."

"Shake it, Smurlee! Do it," Quid jumped up and down in the Sweet Shop aisle between the booths.

Tommy held the box he had collected from the Sunmaker's chapel upside down and shook. A card, pearl gray, business-size fell into his hands. "This must be it!" He read: "The Blue Clue: Dunster's 2 8 1 3."

Grella hugged her shoulders like she always did when she got excited. "This next clue is easy! Where is Room 2813, Blake? Find it on the map."

Blake took the camp map out of the back pocket on his right pants leg. He studied it, then shook his head. "I don't get it. There's no room number that high."

"Let me see the clue," Piney said. "There are spaces between the numbers. Let's go to Room 2, then 8, then 1 and 3 in that order. Maybe there's part of the answer in each room."

"That's an idea," Quid said.

"What's the first one —Room 2?" Tommy asked.

"Croggle's Office. Second room is Counselor Tiddles activity —Room 8," Blake said reading them off the map. "The Counselor's Lounge is next. Finally the Twickle Lab."

"How are we going to get keys for all these rooms?"

"Who needs keys?" Blake pulled a hairpin from a buttoned pocket in his cuff. This will get us in anywhere."

Grella shook her head. "I'm not breaking in and neither are you. All but one of the rooms is usually open and they're empty at some time during each day. The only problem will be Croggle's office."

"Lots of luck. Croggle stays so busy scheduling sessions and planning camp programs that he rarely leaves his office unless there's a camp emergency." Blake said.

"We'll have to get him out with a distraction," Tommy said.

They were silent several minutes.

"I have an idea." Grella jumped up. "We need two people —someone sweet and someone small who have rarely been in trouble. That way in case they get caught they won't be sent home. We can't afford to lose team members." Grella looked at Maryna, then Toodle.

Maryna cowered and tried to shrink into her chair. Everybody crowded around while Grella told them her plan to divert Director Croggle.

Quid whistled, "Brilliant. Toodle can get in."

Toodle beat his chest with his small fists. "I'm Mighty Mr. Toodle. I can do it," he said.

It took some persuading, but Maryna finally agreed to help.

"Hurry. We've only an hour left of today's sessions," Toodle reminded them.

Maryna and Toodle rode the Whoosher to the main floor while the rest of the Silver Team stayed in the room.

Toodle went over the instructions with Maryna, then gently pushed her in the direction of the Director's office.

Maryna walked swiftly to the fire alarm outside the office while Toodle stationed himself a few feet from the Director's office. Toodle slapped his body as flat against the wall as he could.

Suddenly the fire alarm outside Croggle's office jangled shrilly.

"Viola, call the fire department," Director Croggle yelled at his office assistant, as he rushed into the hall to supervise evacuation of the building.

"Where's the fire?" Croggle yelled at the top of his lungs. "Who set off that alarm?"

Toodle hurried up behind careful to stay out of sight. During the noise and chaos Toodle entered Croggle's office. Tommy looked around for somewhere to hide.

Outside campers were streaming out of the wings heading for the front yard.

Croggle saw Maryna midway in the hall a few feet from the fire alarm. Instead of running out with the other campers Maryna seemed to be studying two cement swans outside the window. She stood stiff as an oak tree. "Hmm," Director Croggle said aloud. "You're breathing so heavily I can hear you."

Croggle became instantly suspicious. Having been a Director for eighteen years he knew when something didn't seem right. "Young lady, why did you set off that alarm?"

"Me, sir?"

"Yes. Did you observe a fire in this building that caused you to set it off?" He looked into her eyes and instantly knew the answer.

Croggle whipped out his cell phone and made a call. "Viola, signal false alarm immediately."

Then he turned back to Maryna.

"Maryna, you might have gotten away with it, but you stayed behind. Wanted to see the results, did you?"

Maryna was afraid to open her mouth.

"First violation, is it?"

She nodded.

"Next time don't stand within a few feet of the alarm after it goes off, but there better not be a next time, young lady."

"Yes, sir," she said swiftly.

"Come into my office."

Maryna followed him, but hovered near the door, wondering if Toodle had made it in. Where would he have hidden? Was he in the closet, the bathroom, under the desk? She didn't want to see him.

"Sit down. Tell me, was this a loyalty test as initiation for advanced teamwork? Sometimes that's how these pranks get started."

Maryna perched on the edge of a chair and squiggled, "I wanted to create some excitement. I'm sorry, I truly am." It was all true. Like Grella, Maryna refused to lie ever.

"Do you have any idea how many sessions have been disrupted?"

"No, sir."

"Perhaps you didn't know how serious a violation this is?"

She didn't answer because she did know. Instead she asked, "How did you figure out I did it?"

"It didn't take much."

Then Director Croggle surprised Maryna. He started to laugh. "I'm sorry, excuse me, dear, but you were breathing like a rhinoceros."

Maryna wanted to giggle too, but she was too scared. Whatever her punishment she felt relieved that he didn't sound too mad.

"Now my dear child, someone must have helped you. Tell me who." Croggle was very serious again.

Maryna's voice shook, but she told the truth. "No sir, I set it off alone."

"I know that, but whose idea was it?"

Maryna drew herself up straighter. "I wanted to do it." She would take the punishment herself. After all, she did it, even if Grella had suggested it. Nobody forced her.

"Why?"

"To see if you'd come check what was going on." That was the truth. She didn't need to add the part about Toodle getting into this office. Mr. Toodle wasn't going to hurt anything, only look around.

"This sort of thing can cause serious trouble. Repeat that after me."

She said the words dutifully although her voice shook badly.

Fortunately for Maryna Director Croggle remembered doing a few mischievous things himself as a youth. He noticed how nervous she was. It wouldn't do to have her crying hysterically.

"Now off with you. I won't give you a Dunster's Discharge, only a severe warning, but if there's any further mischief home you go."

"Oh there won't be sir." Maryna couldn't bear to hear that.

After she left Croggle locked his office carefully and left for the day unaware Toodle had squeezed himself behind the supply cabinet.

Maryna raced back to her room and sat on the edge of her bed until her body stopped quivering. Finally she calmed down enough to report to Tommy.

At 6:55 P.M Toodle opened the Director's door for Tommy.

"Where's Grella? I thought she was coming, too," Toodle asked.

"Checking the Twickle Lab. How's it going here?"

"I've been looking on the bookshelves. There's nothing there."

"I'll check the places you might not be able to reach," Tommy paused. "I wonder if the blue clue might glow in the dark?"

"No," Toodle said immediately. "When Croggle left he turned off the lights and I would have seen any blue glow in the dark."

"Maybe it's inside something. Let's be sure we check every nic-nac shelf and pull out all the books. They used the dim light of two tiny flashlights to avoid turning on the overhead light.

There was no blue clue to be seen.

Finally at ten o'clock Toddle said, "I quit. There's nothing here."

"Let's try a little longer, circle the room backwards."

They were on their hands and feet checking the wallboards when the office door creaked. Tommy and Toodle froze. A ray of light came in as the door opened wider.

Tommy crawled under the desk. Toodle dove silently for the open closet.

An eerie sound like grinding filled the darkness. Something or someone had entered.

A subhuman kind of growl followed, then another and another. It almost sounded like a wild animal. Was it Dagta?

Toodle squeezed his body into a little ball. He'd never been so scared in his entire life. Neither Tommy nor Toodle dared look.

Tommy prayed, *Dear Sunmaker, we need help.* Almost instantly he felt a surge of spirit power. He crawled to the opening on his hands and knees and peeked out. A big shadowy figure stood ten feet from him. Whatever, whoever it was, he or she was dressed in a huge black cape. A full rubber hood with eye, nose and mouth slits covered the head.

The figure pulled a gun and said in a threatening voice, "I hear intruders in here. Do you know what happens to intruders at Dunster's? We shoot them."

"Wait!" Tommy jumped up with his arms lifted toward the ceiling. "Don't shoot. We're not armed. We were just looking around."

"We? There's another one?" The caped figure started thrashing around the room.

Tommy ducked back down behind the desk.

The figure looked in the corners of the room, then he stood in front of the closet.

"Come out, so I can shoot you." The creature with the gun growled out the words.

The hair on Tommy's neck stood up. Was it a man?

Toodle pounded on the closet door from the inside. He yelled, "I'm sorry, I'm sorry, don't shoot, please! I'll come out."

The cloaked figure opened the closet door a speck.

Tommy screamed, "Wait! Stop!"

The figure ignored him, stuck the gun in and pulled the trigger.

"Pop, pop," sounded.

Toodle came running out groping his body all over to see where he'd been hit. Tommy couldn't see any blood.

The creature dragged itself over toward the office door and flicked on the lights. Then he threw off his cloak. He came back and sat down at the desk still wearing the rubber hood. Tommy saw that he carried a cassette player under his arm.

Tommy was puzzled. Was this Dagta? Did he know where the clues were hidden? Tommy pressed on his heart to stop its pounding.

The figure whipped off his hood and Tommy gasped, "Director Croggle!"

"I hope this teaches you not to be sneaks, gentlemen! It's one thing to be resourceful and creative, and another to be deceitful. You will lose ten points from your total score, but what's worse you've lowered yourselves by sneaking like this. This clue was a test of integrity as well, and you failed miserably. You could have asked me and you would have been given permission to enter this room without all this deceit."

It was past eleven when Tommy and Toodle finished their apologies and finally crept back to their beds clueless.

Piney was waiting up. "How'd you do?"

"The office was not the room with the blue clue! Don't ask us anything else." Tommy dropped on his bed. "We're exhausted."

"Well, we checked Tiddles' room and the Counselor's Lounge. There's nothing there, either," Piney said. "And Grella hit the Twickle Lab. Nothing! Now what?"

146

"So much for our sequenced room number theory," Tommy said. "There must be another key to this riddle. We'll find it yet."

Chapter 22
Toodle

After his fright in the Director's office, Toodle went straight to the dining hall for a snack. Even though it was close to midnight, he knew he couldn't sleep yet.

Unfortunately Orson holding Migtwee happened to be passing by and saw Toodle sitting alone. He stopped.

Toodle continued smearing his plate with peanut butter. Then he coated the top with jelly and was twirling a piece of bread on top making designs in the sticky surface.

Orson walked over placing his scraggly cat, Migtwee, on his shoulder and glowered at Toodle. "You eat slop!" Orson said. "Hey, Migtwee, what do you think of this?"

Migtwee jumped on a chair and stared at Toodle through hard grey-green eyes.

Toodle felt his heart in his mouth. His skin turned to ice. He tried to ignore Orson, but his fingers shook as he cut the bread with a knife and fork. He took one bite and tried to swallow. The food felt like a rubber ball jammed in his throat.

Usually Toodle hummed while he ate. Not now, not with Orson and Migtwee watching. Toodle liked to imagine himself strong and able to lift 5000-pound weights. He didn't feel strong tonight.

"How about going for a walk?" Orson asked.

"I'm eating," Toodle said remembering Quid's plight. Toodle wondered why his voice sounded like a parakeet's.

"Well, I'll just keep you company here then."

Toodle desperately wished someone were there to help. He looked around. The dining hall was deserted. He gulped.

"Migtwee does what I tell him, Orson said. "You're in luck, Toodle, I'm going to give you a lesson. Some people like to control other people. You must be very nice or they can get quite nasty."

At the mention of his name Migtwee wiggled.

Orson glared at Toodle. "You better do what you're told or else. I'm ready for some entertainment. Let's see you toddle on those little legs," Orson said.

Toddle's face turned the color of a tomato.

Just then Quid happened to come down the hall to the dining room to retrieve the cap he'd forgotten. Instantly he figured out what was happening and called Tommy on his cell phone.

Piney answered and Quid blurted out, "Come quick. Toodle needs help."

Piney said, "We're in bed. We've been busy chasing clues and now we're worn out. Can't you handle Orson?"

Tommy overheard Piney talking.

"Of course he can't handle Orson alone. Where is he? Let's go." Tommy threw clothes at Piney, pulled on his own jeans and shirt and they took off on a run.

"We go just like that?" Piney said huffing. He could hardly keep up.

"Yes, if a friend is in trouble that's what we do. Friends are more important than rest or even solving a mystery."

By the time they reached the cafeteria, Orson had Toodle jammed against the wall and Quid was trying to pull Orson off him.

When they arrived Migtwee screeched and headed off on a run.

Orson let go of Toodle and sneered at Tommy and Piney. "You're lucky. I'm already on probation; I can't risk a fight in here. Otherwise you'd all be chopped chicken when I got through with you."

Toodle dragged himself over to a table. Everybody could see he was trying to hold back tears. "I'm sorry," gulp, "I know you guys are tired. I'm sorry you had to bother."

"Bother! Never! The important thing is, are you okay?"

Piney looked less than happy to be there, but was wise enough to keep silent.

"Toodle, for the next couple of days," Tommy said, "I want you to eat all your meals with one of us. Don't go off alone between activities either. Got that? You're an important member of our team and we can't risk losing you!"

Toodle felt his chunks of fear being sliced into small pieces. Maybe this hadn't been such a totally awful, miserable time after all. He had no idea he mattered this much to his friends. And tomorrow, why he might be able to help his team solve this mystery! Provided he stayed away from Orson.

Chapter 23
Living Art

"Stop, I dropped my scarf!" Grella yelled.

Tommy, Grella, and Blake were hanging on the rope in the Wind Whoosher the next day, one behind the other heading for a Slap/Dash match.

"We can't stop," Blake said, although he felt sorry for Grella. He hated it when he lost anything. "You can get it back from Lost and Found. Everything lost gets turned in there. Don't feel too bad."

"The only thing I'd really miss if I lost it is my Red Notebook," Tommy said, "with all my special notes and drawings and, of course, my marked-up Book of Holy Words is special, too." He kept both in his room under his bed in a locked metal case. That was in case Piney's lizard got at them and started chewing.

"Where's Lost and Found?" Tommy asked.

"It's a huge crate in the garage. On Saturday Hickenstein opens the crate for twenty-four hours. You have to wait until then if you've lost something. What doesn't get claimed he sells at the end of the season." Blake shouted through the wind.

It turned out they didn't have to worry about getting the scarf back after all. A loud shredding noise was followed by an alarm going off.

"Oh no! Your scarf must have caught in the Wind Whoosher ball mechanism."

The Wind Whoosher came to a screeching stop suspended in the air between floors. Buzzzzz! Snap! The lights went out. The Whoosher couldn't move up or down.

"Now what?" Grella said sounding both mad and worried.

"We're going to fall, that's what," Blake said.

"No, we're not! The emergency air flow will hold us in place," Tommy said, "but the pulley can't move up or down. "

"Let's climb the pulley to the next floor," Blake said.

"It's too hard to climb the pulley to go between floors, with its sharp hooks," Tommy explained. "You must have a flashlight in your pants' pocket Blake?"

"Sure do, two." Seconds later he flashed circles of light on the sidewall. He and Tommy made out a tiny square door on the sidewall of the elevator channel. They looked at it in surprise, then at each other. "Grella, there's a door here!"

The door was a little over three feet away. They had to stretch way out to touch it.

"That's weird. Where could it go?" Grella yelled from below. "There's no floor here."

"It's probably only a closet with a control panel, but we'll check, it's a good spot to hide a clue," Tommy said. He wished he had his Red Notebook now to check the dimensions of the Wind Whoosher channel. If he had his measurements he might know where this door went."

Blake leaned way over and pushed on the door. "It has to open in because the elevator channel is so narrow, but it won't budge." He tried to plunge his elbow at it.

Grella said, "Let me climb past you Blake, I'm smaller. If you swing me maybe I can get my legs on the door and kick it in."

"Good idea," Tommy said. "I'll hold the rope steady. Carefully change places. I'll brace my legs against the opposite wall."

Blake grabbed Grella's hand with his free arm.

He swung Grella toward the door. She gave a mighty kick with both her legs.

Nothing happened. She clutched the rope again.

"It won't work," Blake said impatiently. "And I don't want to stay here forever."

"Someone will hear the alarm and come," Tommy reassured Blake. He didn't say what he was thinking —that it could be hours until the Whoosher was fixed.

Blake said. "This better not take too long." Sweat began to form on his forehead. He disliked being stuck anywhere.

"Let's try another kick," Tommy said. "This time, Blake, swing the pulley rope out and I'll kick with Grella. Blake, you hold Grella steady."

"But we'll all slam into the wall," Blake said. Sweat was dripping down his nose.

"Not if we get the door open." Tommy propelled his legs karate style.

"Plumph!!" The door shot open and Tommy went in with it.

Grella had no choice, but to follow him. Blake entered third.

Grella teased, "Hey, Blake. Do you know what just happened? You weren't first. See, it's not so bad." Grella picked herself up and straightened her shorts and tank top.

"Let's not discuss it," Blake said wiping his forehead on his sleeve.

Tommy stared at the dimly lit gray corridor ahead of them. "A tiny door, a big hall. Where does this go?"

"Weird," Blake said, walking ahead of them. "This isn't a control closet. It's the entrance to another floor. Where are we?"

"Let's see what's here." Tommy pushed Blake. "It seems we're on part of an unnumbered floor."

"There's no unnumbered floor."

"Well we've whooshed past two and haven't come to three." Tommy's face brightened. "This floor isn't on the map Croggle gave me. Nor is it on the map I made myself. I know where there could be missing rooms. But a missing floor? It must be suspended between one and two. Remember the ceiling is two-floors-high in the cafeteria. This would be the other end."

"So it's only suspended on the west wing?" Grella asked.

"I don't care how it got built – I don't like it. I want to leave, this is eerie," Blake said.

"But wait, what a great hiding place," Tommy said. "What if our Blue Clue is hidden here?"

"Yeah and what if Orson Gartini is already here," Blake's voice quivered.

"Stay close. Let's walk single file," Tommy ordered.

"I've got another flashlight," Blake said, pulling it from his left thigh pocket. He flashed the light along the wall until they found a light switch. Grella flicked it on.

Suddenly the sidewalls were flooded with squeamish-green fluorescent light. They found themselves in a kind of art gallery.

"Look at all the pictures," Blake said.

"Did you ever see so many oil paintings in your life?" Tommy could scarcely believe his eyes.

"I bet there's an envelope hanging on one of these pictures or behind it." Grella said. "Why keep this hidden unless there's a clue here." Her voice got more excited.

"Don't count on it," Tommy said. "I can't imagine a clue in a place that would be almost impossible to find. And it's supposed to be blue remember."

Grella walked eagerly down the center of the room. "My turn to find a clue. You guys stay here. I'll explore."

"This green light is making me sick," Blake said.

"I'll investigate with you, Grella," Tommy said. "If anyone comes to rescue us, Blake, use your tooter to let us know," Tommy ordered.

"Nice and loud," Grella added. She was already entering the next room. Let's see what's in here, Tommy."

"Nothing but farm scene pictures," he said.

They entered the next room. About twenty-five portraits of men and women hung on the walls.

"This is a regular museum," Grella said.

"But there's something different about these pictures," Tommy said. "Have you noticed?"

"What?"

"When I stand in front of a picture it's like what's going on in the frame is happening right now and the people come to life for a few seconds. The figures in this picture start to move."

"Are you sure?"

"Try it for yourself." They moved toward the next picture. "See this farmer plowing his field."

"Weird! How do they do that?" Grella's eyes widened.

"Here's a sign," Tommy read slowly, 'Living Art.'"

"What's that?" Grella screwed up her nose like she always did when thinking really hard.

"I don't know." Tommy went closer to one of the pictures. "Look at this! Some of the canvases have one to three inch burn holes, as if something burned the picture but only part of it."

"Weird?" Grella walked over to another picture.

As Tommy studied a canvas of colonial life the lady cooking over a wood stove began to age before his eyes. She went from a young mother to a grandmother. Then there was a poof of smoke and then nothing but a burn hole where she had been.

Grella was looking at a woman sewing a dress for her daughter. "Tommy, come here."

Tommy pulled out his timer when he approached the picture. While he stood there in front of it the people in it started moving. When he walked past they stopped and were now older.

"This is the strangest art I've ever seen," Tommy said.

Grella whistled. "It's like they're living and dying as we watch. Living Art."

"But if we don't come too close they stay the same," Tommy observed.

Tommy wandered off looking at the front of the pictures and behind them for a Mystery Card clue envelope.

Eventually he came to the end of the hall. Another door led to a small closet not unlike where they'd entered. There was a trap door on the floor. He lifted it. Beneath he could see Dunster campers wandering into the cafeteria for snacks.

He walked back to Grella who was looking at a baby becoming a child, then a man, an old man and then poof. Nothing remained but another burned out hole in a canvas.

"Unless you come within two feet of the picture, it remains lifeless," Tommy said, "I measured the distance back until it stopped moving."

"Let's stop looking, we're destroying them," Grella said. "This place needs to stay hidden."

"Hey guys, I'm over here," Blake yelled.

"Where Blake?"

They followed Blake's voice to a little alcove where he was examining a Civil War picture.

156

"Tommy, see the canon in this war picture. They're dragging it up the hill to put it into position to fire. Now it's being loaded."

"It's what? Blake, get away from that."

"No, wait. I think they're about to fire."

"We've got to get out of here before it goes off."

"I want to see it. This is amazing! Leave me alone."

"No, it's too dangerous. We don't know what will happen."

"You're not my boss!"

"No, but I'm your friend and I won't let you do something stupid or dangerous." With that Tommy yanked on Blake's arm as hard as he could and dragged him.

Blake moaned. He tried to slow Tommy down. Tommy wouldn't listen. Grella ran along behind them.

When they reached the spot where they'd left the Whoosher. Tommy grabbed the pulley, still holding Blake's arm. Then he swung the rope toward Grella.

"Let's go."

"Pray that it's been fixed. Put the ball down for the whoosh."

As the Wind Whoosher took off they heard an explosion behind them.

"Whew!" Tommy said, "We barely got whooshed away in time!"

Grella's voice was shaking. "Why blow up all those pictures?"

"Maybe it didn't, hopefully it was only the canon we heard, but we couldn't take a chance," Tommy said.

"Let's go back and look." Blake said looking miffed at being pulled away.

"We'll return after we research this," Tommy consoled him.

"Darn, I thought surely a clue would be there," Grella said.

The next day they met with Counselor Artur their mystery adviser. He listened carefully but found Tommy, Blake and Grella's story about Living Art impossible to believe. He stalked out of his office to consult immediately with Croggle who came back at his heels. The Director's face looked stern and he was frowning. This time his anger was for real.

"Yes, indeed there is an art hall. It's an experiment started by Counselor Zeller before he became ill. No one must know about this until his pictures can be stopped from ultimate destruction. Zeller knows how to start them living but has found no way to turn them off."

"You mean," Grella said, still amazed at what she'd seen, "that the pictures begin as beautiful creations?"

"Yes, but then the people in them grow old and die when someone stares at them and then there's ugly holes in the canvas where they once were," the Director said.

"Why can't he fix them?" she asked.

"He's been urr, rather ill. We're hoping once he's better, he can. Until then we're keeping the art hidden. We can't have dangerous pictures being seen that we can't control. We thought we'd already destroyed all the pictures with guns and explosives, but we missed the one that Blake found."

Croggle glared at the members of the Silver Team. "We protect the work of our staff. He'd be a laughing stock if the pictures are seen as they are now," Croggle said. "Now back to your dorm quarters, Dunnies."

"Who's he calling a dummy?" Blake joked once they were out of the office. "We find a hidden art gallery, I'd say we're pretty smart."

"Now what?" Grella asked.

Blake said, "I'm researching this clue alone. You guys are slowing me down. I've got some code book resources." Blake patted the biggest pocket sewn on the outside of his pants.

Piney ran up in the hall, his face red as the inside of a watermelon. "Where were you? We lost today's Slap/Dash match because we didn't have enough back up. You could at least have let me know you weren't coming."

"You're absolutely right." *Never argue with an angry man,* Tommy thought, *especially when you're in the wrong. He can't hear you.* Tommy's Dad had taught him that. Wait until he's spouted his anger. Then if there's anything true that you can agree with or need to apologize for, do it right away.

Piney huffed a few more times, then drew back and glared, "Well?"

"Well what?"

"Why didn't you come?"

"You know we must have a good reason," Tommy said. "We would never miss a game on purpose, especially when camp time is so precious." Tommy explained about Grella's scarf, the broken Wind Whoosher.

"Why didn't you say so in the first place?" Piney complained. "Have you heard how the team made out studying the Mystery Card numbers 2813 as a code?"

"No, but last I saw," Tommy said, "Blake had books on encrypted code and Navaho code sticking out of his pockets."

"Somebody better come up with an idea," Grella said. "We're running out of time."

Chapter 24
The Golden Stone

The next morning fog thick as tar coated Dunster's.

Piney awoke at seven. "I think I have it!" He jumped out of bed and started pacing.

Tommy was already up and pulling on his socks. "Have what? Quiet down. You'll wake the entire wing."

Piney knocked three times on the wall of their room adjacent to Quid and Blake's room.

The brothers came rushing in, Quid still in his red and black checkered pajamas. Blake was dressed except for his shirt.

"What's up?"

Piney repeated, "I know," raising his fist in the air. "I figured it out."

"Stop babbling and tell us," Blake insisted with his usual impatience.

"I bounced around in bed all night like a ball on a tennis racket. It was worth it. I awoke with the answer!"

"To what?" Quid asked, still sleepy.

Piney looked at Quid as if he'd lost his nose. "To the clue 2813 of course!" Was Quid the biggest dummy he'd ever seen?

"Tell us!" Blake shouted the words.

"The numbers get added together to make the room number —2 plus 8 plus 1 plus 3."

That sounds too simple, duh," Blake mocked.

"Yeah! Remember this is Dunster's Great Unsolved Mystery. They'd never do something that easy," Quid said.

"Wait," Tommy said. "Maybe they would. The heart of any mystery is simple."

Blake turned up his nose. "What's that supposed to mean?"

"Truth is simple," Tommy said, "not complicated —clear and easy. Once a mystery is revealed it's seems easy, but that's only because you know the answer."

"Straight and simple —let's check Piney's idea, hurry up and tell us," Blake said with his usual lack of patience.

"Okay." Quid asked Blake for the map in his pants pocket.

"I don't have to look at it, I remember," Tommy said, "room two plus eight plus one plus three equals fourteen. Room 14 is the Music Hall."

Piney said, "Then the clue must be there."

"Wait a minute! Blake mumbled, the blue clue could be the music itself."

"I'm with you on this. Remember that part of the clue, 'follow your feet'" Quid said. "There's music from the South called Blues and people dance to it. I do too. Let's check the Blues music."

"Take fifteen minutes to finish dressing and grab some juice and toast. We'll meet at the Music Hall," Tommy said.

Tommy arrived first and caught Counselor Moovit, the music counselor, leaving the Music Hall. Tommy inquired about the Blues music.

"Yes, we have Blues sheet music and CD's. They're in the Blues file drawer. I'll show you where I keep them. He led him to the wooden file cabinet in the back of the room. "I'm so glad you're showing interest and expanding your appreciation of music, Mr. Smurlee. You'll find some excellent piano selections here."

"Yes sir," Tommy said.

"Close the door when you leave."

"Yes, sir."

Shortly after Counselor Moovit left, Blake and Quid arrived. Tommy had expected to go through every CD and piece of sheet music, but didn't have to.

Inside the cabinet behind the blues music they found a stone the size of a fist, flecked with gold and a packet of eight envelopes tied with a blue ribbon. In the Silver Team envelope there was a picture of a gold-flecked stone with rays shooting out from it.

"What's this supposed to mean?" Blake asked.

"The clue must be the stone. Stones are hard, stones are rough." Quid was thinking out loud.

"And some stones are smooth and shiny gold," Blake corrected.

"That's it! I'd guess it's something about the gold," Quid said.

"Guesses aren't good enough," Tommy insisted. "We need to use logic." He turned the stone over again. "See those scratches.

Tommy whipped something out of his shirt pocket. Let me put on my magnifying headband." Tommy looked more closely. "There's tiny letters etched along the edges."

"What do they say?" Quid asked.

"It's hard to make out. Wait, the first word is 'where.'" Tommy studied the stone some more. Then he read aloud, "Where do I come from?"

"What's that supposed to mean?" Piney asked.

"Think! These are thought clues!" Tommy said.

"I'm trying," Blake said.

162

"All stones come from earth, but gold flecks, gold, golden. Wait!" Tommy said. "Counselor Golden teaches Mysteries of Earth? And stones come from the earth."

"That fits! I think you've got it. At least it's worth a try," Blake said.

"I hope so, we're running out of time. Orson will be on our tail," Quid reminded them.

"Right." Blake glared at Tommy who was busily staring at the ceiling. "Our team wasted a lot of time in Croggle's office."

"I had a dream three days ago," Tommy said. "Angels the size of dinosaurs were guarding a chest with fiery swords so Dagta couldn't reach it."

"What was in it?" Blake asked, his eyes wide.

"I woke up before I could open it."

"What does that have to do with Golden?" Quid asked.

"Doesn't Counselor Golden keep a big Nature Chest in his room for objects that campers collect? Maybe that's where this stone came from."

"So?" Quid said.

"I think we need to see what else is in that chest!" Tommy jumped up. "Is anybody on our team taking his session?"

"Not this week," Blake said after reviewing a copy of every camper's schedules he took from his pants pocket.

"Grella's doing research on worms. I heard her say she was going to interview Counselor Golden."

"Good. I'll go with her," Quid offered.

"No. Let her try this alone. It will make up for the Hidden Garden," Tommy said, "I'll tell her we need her help when I see her in the Monster Session."

Chapter 25
Wishkowski

Piney and Tommy were finishing their first dream of the day just as Counselor Wishkowski stuck his head into the dream lab. First dreams were free choice today. Tommy had chosen to ride a dolphin in a small bay with five other dolphins.

Piney chose one of his usual successful sporting events. He scored 65 at the Master's Golf Tournament in Georgia. He had a huge grin. "I got around the course so fast that I squeezed in a second round and then some football."

That's what got him into trouble.

Counselor Wishkowski gasped when he saw the crumpled sheets and twisted blankets on Piney's cot.

"I told you no wild dreams, Piney Putilla!"

"But I was quarterbacking in the Super Bowl and we won!" Piney beamed.

"Get that bed straightened up. If this happens again you're going into the nightmare unit where such behavior is acceptable!"

The Counselor turned to the entire group and said in a softer voice, "Campers, I have a surprise for you. We're using zoo special effects today for the next dream mod."

"Again?" Piney objected. Zoo effects were Counselor Wishkowski's favorite and he used them more than Piney liked.

Wishkowski turned on a tape of animal sounds. It played softly in the background as Tommy settled down on his cot. He couldn't fall asleep immediately, but finally he did.

A computer software program sent animal smells into his nostrils. After a few minutes Tommy dreamt he was in the jungle. Being around the animals reminded him of his Mom and Dad in Africa. Even though he stayed with his Grandma and Grandpa most summers after he turned six and was old enough for school, before that Tommy spent most of every year in the jungle with his parents.

It was good to be back among the lions, tigers and elephants. The screech of the monkeys and the roar of elephants had been his crib music as a baby. It made him long for his parents.

Miss you Mom, Miss you, Dad, Tommy thought, and blinked quickly.

"You coming, Tommy?" Piney called back from ten feet ahead. How did Piney get into his dream?

"Yeah, wait up," Tommy yelled

"Let's check out the snakes!"

Together they watched snakes being fed. Tommy missed his own pet boa, Kia. At least he knew Kia was being well cared for in its cage in his grandparent's basement. Keeping Kia stocked with white mice took a lot of his allowance, even if Dad sometimes gave him money to help.

Tommy still spent some of his allowance on mystery books and research equipment for his experiments, but food for his boa, Kia, came first.

Piney's voice drifted through Tommy's mind.

Suddenly Tommy was awake. "What a way to end a dream," Tommy said, "With a vision of a boa constrictor, just like mine at home."

"Grella wasn't so lucky, I hear," Blake said pushing his way past Tommy and Piney to be first out the door.

"What do you mean?" Tommy asked.

"She started screaming during a nightmare in the cubicle next to me. The counselor sent her into the chamber for a fear spin."

"Oh, no! She gets even more frightened when she takes the fear spin," Piney said.

"What's the fear spin?" Tommy asked.

"I wish there was another way," Blake said. "But it'll work, she'll be fine."

"I've never heard of it." Tommy began to sweat and his hands grew clammy. "Will somebody please tell me what you're talking about?"

"In the spin you think of the worst possible thing that could happen, then pretend it's happening, and decide how you'd deal with it. It's supposed to make you feel brave afterward," Piney said. "Sometimes it does, but not always."

"Poor Grella." Tommy shuddered.

"Doesn't make sense," Blake added.

"It's Counselor Boota's theory. He's testing it out on the campers. Pretty scary," Piney said. "Who knows how long she'll be in there."

"If you see her, tell her I'll pray for her," Tommy said. "I hope she makes it out in time for our Monster Activity," Tommy said.

"Yeah, sure. Like prayer's going to help," Piney said. He shuffled off to his next activity mumbling. "I can never get a good sports dream when Wishkowski programs those disgusting animal smells."

"Wait up," Tommy called after him. "For this session where monsters prowl, I want to walk in with a friend!"

Chapter 26
Monster Mania

The campers in the Monster Mania session sat alert and perfectly still in the Great Hall waiting for the counselor to arrive.

Counselor Wirtler charged in wearing a gray rubber facemask with black, fake hair around the ears and a beard. His hands were covered with huge rubber paws.

Good afternoon," he snarled. "We're using the Great Hall for our activity session today because we need lots of room as you'll see shortly." He rubbed his paws together and made a deep growling sound. "Let's begin."

"Why is he dressed like that?" Maryna asked Tommy.

"I have no idea. Scary though, isn't it?"

"Take a note paper and a pencil from the box by the door." The Counselor began to lecture. "Monsters come in several forms. There are mythical monsters, magical monsters and malicious people who pose as monsters. Before we go on, where do you suppose the word 'monster' comes from?"

Nobody answered. No camper had ever thought about it.

The Counselor pointed to Quid with a massive black nail, "Look 'monster' up in the dictionary, Mr. Hammond. We'll wait."

Moments later Quid read, "An animal or plant of abnormal form; a threatening force, a person of unnatural or extreme ugliness."

"Yes, and there's one more," Counselor Wirtler said, "my definition is, a creature who's extremely different in development or behavior. That's the meaning we'll use, although the others are correct, too. Write them down."

Pencils sped across notebook paper.

"Next questions: Where do we most often find monsters? And how are they useful?"

"I don't know and I don't want to know," Grella whispered to Maryna.

Counselor Wirtler overheard her. "Well, you must know, Miss Weller! Listen carefully. Monsters are featured in books and movies made to frighten. To create terror the words and special effects of these stories must be just right."

"Makes sense," Tommy said.

"That's the kind of story you will write today. To inspire your imagination everyone will wear a monster costume."

Orson grinned. "I can't wait," he said to Toodle. "I hope I don't scare you. I'd never want to do that." Orson leaned so close that Toodle felt Orson's breath on his neck.

Toodle moved to the opposite side of the room.

Counselor Wirtler's voice droned on. "Soon we'll leave the Great Hall and go into the mask and costume room where you may make your selections. Everyone will dress in a private dressing room. You may keep your mask on twenty-four hours only. If you leave here still in costume, you must not use your real voice until removing your costume."

"Why not, Counselor Wirtler?" Maryna asked.

"My dear, your voice is an identity giveaway."

"But what if we want to talk to each other?" Maryna wanted to know.

"You'll communicate by writing."

"Doesn't writing also give away our identity? Everyone's penmanship is different," Quid said.

"Good point!" Counselor Wirtler said. "I can tell you've been in the Orderly Thunking Session."

Quid loved praise. "Well, I often know who's sending me a note. It's not tough to recognize handwriting."

"Don't you think I've thought of that?" Counselor Wirtler said huffily. "You may speak only by think-padding on a pocket Think Pad."

The campers looked at each other bewildered.

"What's that?" Quid murmured.

"I will explain as you get into your costumes, campers."

Wirtler asked Toodle to help pass out what looked like small flat boxes. "These are your Think Pads. You hold your hand on them and think of the message or story you want to write. Then you may share your message or story by sending it electromagnetically to whomever you wish. Only one thought at a time or your thoughts will jumble and nothing will go through. Is that clear?"

"Neat!" Quid said.

Tommy examined the Think Pad silently.

"Any other questions?" Counselor Wirtler asked.

Tommy raised his hand. "How will we tell the Think Pad where to send the message or story?"

"Excellent! I was wondering if someone would ask."

"Yeah," Orson, interrupted, "I was just about to."

The Counselor frowned at Orson and continued.

"First think of the person you wish to contact. When you can see this person clearly in your mind, put your hand on the pad and send your message or story. The pad will pick up your visual vibrations. Once your message is sent the person who is the receiver will hear three beeps to alert them to your incoming message."

"Amazing." Tommy whistled.

"Grella, test the procedure please. Say hello and how are you to Maryna."

Grella and Maryna went through the process while everyone watched.

"It works perfectly," Maryna said.

"Are we ready?" Counselor Wirtler said.

Tommy raised his hand again. "How will we retrieve the message or story?"

"No one has asked that yet. My compliments, Camper Smurlee. In order to read what's sent to you, turn your Think Pad to the backside, and put your hand on the lower half. All the messages or stories sent to you will be printed one by one on the screen. Now, let's start!"

The counselor drew himself up to his almost seven-foot height. Counselor Wirtler was easily the tallest counselor at Dunster's.

"This is fantastic," Orson said, glaring at Grella. "I can think any ugly thoughts about you I want and send them in a story straight to your pad."

"Like I care!" Grella shot back.

"I'll be looking over your shoulders," the counselor warned, "and checking that you're using this new Dunster's invention properly. If we're successful with our tests we'll be passing the Think Pad invention on to our State Department. If you misuse the Think Pad you forfeit your privilege to carry one."

Maryna thought of silly monster jokes she could share and giggled.

Counselor Wirtler glared at Maryna. "There is nothing funny about mystery or monsters, young woman."

"Sorry, sir."

"One more thing, the use of monster make-up on your hands isn't allowed during our session."

A bell jangled.

"Now we'll enter the studio where you will make your monster costume selections. After you put on your costumes rejoin the campers in the Great Hall. Then write your monster stories standing or sitting at the large tables. Being in the presence of one another in full costume will stimulate your imaginations.

When you finish, you may share your stories with one another using your Think Pads. Send them to me also though. I expect excellent stories. I'll be entering the best in the Worldwide Monster Story Competition. The winner gets a free week at any summer camp in the country although I doubt there's a better one than Dunster's anywhere. Remember you may keep your Think Pads and your costumes only twenty-four hours."

Blake rushed to the head of the line. Toodle blocked him and wouldn't let him pass at first, but Blake shoved Toodle a couple of times until he fell.

"Blake, can't you get over this?" Grella complained. "You're so rude!"

She helped Toodle up.

"I'm trying. Sorry, Toodle," Blake apologized. "The Sunmaker's helping me work on this. I am getting a little better, I think."

The counselor walked to the back of the room. "I'll wait for you here, campers. Now select your costumes."

The campers began to sort through the collection. An odor of mustiness and rubber seeped into the room as boxes and barrels that had been sealed since last year's camp were opened.

Tommy picked through masks on the side shelves. He finally selected a Werewolf mask.

Blake sidled up to him wearing a Frankenstein costume. "Can't you find something better than that, Tommy?"

"What's wrong with a Werewolf?"

"It's so common."

Tommy looked at Blake again. "I suppose Frankenstein isn't common?" Tommy picked another mask with three heads, all green, with magenta, orange and green colored hair, and eyeballs as big as eggs. "How about this, Quid?"

"Perfect! Don't show anyone else. I'm going to be a walking corpse in a body bag with legs. At least we'll know each other."

Counselor Wirtler called out, "Final selections, now, hurry into your dressing rooms. You may still speak in here. Use of the Think Pads begins in the Great hall. Remember they only work when you're within twenty-five feet of one another."

While they put on their costumes, Counselor Wirtler gave more instructions. "Write your stories immediately. You may return your costume as soon as you finish or you may keep it the full twenty-four hours, but no mystery work on the Great Unsolved Mystery may be done while in costume. Remember if the mystery is still unsolved by the end of camp it's declared forever unsolvable. You don't want that in camp history do you? Get your stories written promptly, then return to your sleuthing. Be creative, and always use time efficiently."

A long, low growl filled the air.

"Stop, stop!" Counselor Wirtler yelled. "I will not allow fear in here. No growling is allowed, until you're back in the Great Hall."

"Look at me, Counselor, I'm the Headless Horseman," Maryna said.

"I don't need to see you. Go into the Great Hall when you're ready."

About twenty minutes, thirty for those applying make-up too, the campers straggled into the semi-dark Great Hall. A girl in the front row almost swooned when the monster standing beside her howled at her.

Counselor Wirtler stood at the door blocking his vision by turning his head sideways until they'd all passed.

"I believe he's a bit scared," Tommy whispered to Quid.

"That's ridiculous," Quid said.

"Oh yeah?" Tommy knew fear when he saw it. He'd worked hard enough with the Sunmaker to overcome his own.

"Use your Think Pad now, we don't want to be disqualified," Tommy reminded Quid.

"Thanks, I forgot," Quid said.

A creature lunged toward them wearing a long red cape over red pants. He carried a brass spear. Piney signaled them with a thumbs up. Tommy recognized him by the ring he always wore on his right hand.

Piney's hands and face were greased red—even his hair had been dusted red. Big black circles ringed his eyes and circled his arms too.

Once the campers were all back in the Great Hall, Counselor Wirtler said, "You're on your own now." He slammed the door behind him. They heard a lock clicking into place on his office door.

"Where's Orson? Does anybody have an idea what his costume is so we'll know him?" Tommy think-padded to Piney.

"No idea," Piney answered.

Tommy checked with the rest of his team. No one knew for sure what Orson was wearing but Blake saw a knight in full armor lumber over to a table and set up his Think Pad. "I think this might be him."

But it wasn't. Orson sat in the back in a costume that had a horse's head with the body of a locust. He decided to send messages now and write his story later.

Orson think-padded two words to Smurlee, "Give up." And to Blake, "Loser." Quid opened his Think Pad to the message, "Disappear forever, why don't you?"

The campers near Orson heard a sick laugh and saw his horse's head begin to shake.

Grella pushed long scraggly black hair from her ghostly white facemask because it covered her eyes. She read her Think Pad. "Hi Ugly. All my hate, Love, Orson." She was still getting over her fear spin. She began to tremble.

Blake, in a body bag that had green slime where a heart should be, think-padded to Tommy, "Now what?"

"Now we write the best monster stories we can and get out of here before any of them come true. Orson could attack any of us and get away with it in his disguise."

Tommy created a story about a friendly monster, one who helped children who were homesick to fly to their parent's side wherever they were.

He finished his story and turned in his costume.

"This better be good, young man," Counselor Wirtler said. "You're one of the first ones done."

"Yes sir, I mean I hope so."

Tommy hurried back to his dorm room to check his computer. Monster Mania was exciting at first because it was a new activity, but Tommy had enough new experiences at the moment. Should he skip his next session? He wanted time alone to record the past days in his Red Notebook. Plus he was expecting his grandparents' e-mail.

More than anything he wanted to be home watching the birds feeding at one of the ten feeders in Grandma and Grandpa Smurlee's back yard while he drank one of Grandpa's chocolate milk shakes and ate some of Grandma's pecan dainty cookies. He felt an ache inside his chest when he thought of his grandparents.

Even the thrill of solving the Mystery didn't excite him tonight.

Get a grip, he told himself. Victory is within reach. He couldn't skip his next session. Tommy dug deep into himself for more strength and endurance. Feeling a little better, he followed Blake to an Unknown, called Encouragement Lab.

On the way Tommy heard a strange voice speak to him out of nowhere. Or maybe it was a thought from his brain. Tommy couldn't be sure. It asked him if he was getting tired of looking at the back of Blake's head.

What kind of dumb question is that? Tommy thought. Then the voice said, "Get Blake behind you. Why should Blake always be first? You deserve to be in front, you're the team leader."

So what! Tommy shivered. Where were these thoughts coming from? Drubbins? Downers? Dagta?

No more! This nasty thinking could get him into trouble. Why give Dagta an opening into his brain? No way! He replaced the bad thoughts about Blake with positive ones and decided to be extra nice to him instead.

"Hey Blake," Tommy said, drawing up next to him, "I decided to come to this session after all instead of staying in my room to rest. I'm glad you're here too. Want to sit together?"

"Yeah, sure! You're going to like this lab. It's a better pick-me-up than Counselor Doolicky's pickle quick-lift juice.

They perched on stools at a table and put on headphones and eyewear programmed with tapes.

Tommy stared at the changing scenes around him — sunsets, sunrise, mountain mornings.

"Counselor Hapkins controls everything from that glassed-in control station in the center of the room," Blake said.

Tommy and Blake spoke their password into the mouthpiece attached to the headphone set and then heard special a message directed to each of them, "You're never alone."

This must be what the Sunmaker's voice sounds like, Tommy felt sure. "Don't be scared," he heard. "I'm with you always."

Tommy breathed deeply and relaxed.

"Pray, then trust." The messages continued. "Cast all your cares upon me."

When they were almost through, Blake emptied all his pockets on the table and sorted his spoons, scissors, tap, booklets, kneepads, nose plugs and all sorts of things. There must have been at least sixty items. He cleaned, repaired, and even threw some away. "I feel so together when I leave here. Isn't it great?"

Suddenly the messages changed. "You're an idiot." and "No one likes you." and "You've never been loved."

The scenes changed too. Hurricanes, tornadoes, trees falling from lightning appeared one after another on the screen.

Counselor Hapkins came running out of the control room. "This lab is closed the rest of the day. Technical problems. I'm sorry, campers."

"What happened?" Tommy asked the counselor as they filed out.

"Every now and then Dagta gets into the sound and sight system. Try to remember only the first messages you heard. We're switching you over to the Kinet activity instead. I'm sure you'll find it very pleasant." Counselor Hapkins shooed them out.

What is going on at Dunster's Tommy wondered.

Chapter 27
The Kinet Room

Blake, Grella, Quid and Tommy went directly to The Kinet activity, short for kinesthetic. The room where it was held looked like a small movie theater complete with computer stations. A huge movie screen filled one entire wall.

"You're up first, Tommy Smurlee," Counselor Pringle, a small, wiry man announced from his seat in the first row.

"Watch closely, campers. Tommy, stand in the chalk circle here so the sensor can pick up your image and scan it into the computer. The rest of you watch the large screen or you can see Tommy's internal image at one of the computer stations."

Instantly Tommy's on-screen body swayed on the movie theater screen in rhythm to a Spanish song he'd never heard before. *Wow, if only Grandma and Grandpa could see me now,* Tommy thought. Both his grandparents loved music and often danced around the living room, but never like this.

Tommy had never seen a picture of the inside of his body, let alone a display of his shape on a full-size movie screen. His life-size body form was projected in white, his bones glowed green.

As Tommy watched swirls, like circles inside circles, about three inches in diameter, thousands of them, surrounded the outline of his bodily shape and zinged against him. They felt wonderful.

Suddenly the swirls switched to hundreds of three-inch squares that slid around him and slapped gently against his green bones on the screen. His body felt like it was being zapped with energy. He knew it was his own body on the screen because every time he lifted his arm the arm on the screen moved identically.

"This is all about touch and movement. Those squares are the kinets, tiny moving forces," Counselor Pringle said excitedly. "Watch, Smurlee! You're getting the daggers next. And I'm moving your image over and putting up the rest of the campers next to you one by one."

On the screen thousands of tiny arrows bounced off Tommy's bones. He felt little pricks everywhere. "Ouch," he said.

"Stop the projector!" a camper yelled concerned Tommy was getting hurt.

"It's okay," Tommy said. They don't hurt."

"The balls are coming next. They feel soothing," Grella said.

"Why are you giving me vibrations from all these shapes?" Tommy asked Counselor Pringle.

"They bring harmony and energy to your body, they balance you." The Counselor stopped talking to let him enjoy the experience fully.

"It doesn't last, unfortunately." Blake explained in technical jargon that the vibrations were only temporarily soothing.

"Tommy, isn't it wonderful though —Counselor Pringle's experimenting? I find it relaxing, although there's no real purpose, is there Counselor?" Grella asked.

"Grella, excuse me, you have that wrong. Relaxation is necessary," the Counselor said. "It has a very important purpose. Having time with nothing to do but think is vital."

"There's never a lack of ideas to think about, not for me anyway," Quid said, hopping around to see his bones hop on the screen. "And moving helps me think."

"It's true my doing nothing time is sometimes my very best thinking time," Tommy said.

"However you think best, remember to plan time for thinking and resting every day," Counselor Pringle suggested.

"A life without thinking is a useless life," Quid quoted.

Tommy said, "I'd like to have this activity every day."

"Can't," Grella corrected, "Kinet Room is only open on Tuesdays and Thursdays. Wish we could though. Best of all, Orson never comes in here. His body is so big, I don't know if they'd have enough zingers for him."

She looked up as Piney came running in. "I've been looking all over for you. My lizard's dead, " he moaned. "I loved my lizard. I'm gonna get the guy who did this. He drowned him. It had to be Gartini! Who else? He's gonna pay."

"Wait," Tommy yelled. "You can't get even, only the Sunmaker is allowed to take vengeance. Remember?"

"I'm going to pulverize that guy."

"No, you're not." Grella shoved his shoulders with her tiny, but forceful fists. Piney let himself fall into a chair.

"You don't understand," Piney said.

"Yes I do, but vengeance is the wrong answer. First thing we do," said Grella, "is ask the Sunmaker to deal with Orson."

"Whaaaat?" Piney jumped up.

"You heard me. That's what I did, when Orson ate my grasshoppers," Grella answered.

"Well, that didn't help! Orson's still at his old tricks!"

"Sometimes change takes time. It doesn't mean the Sunmaker's not working," Grella insisted shaking her finger at Piney. "In the meantime protect yourself and your stuff as best you can. Don't be a fool."

Piney stuck his chin in the air and walked to the door. "I'll think about it, that's all, got it?" Then he charged out.

"I better follow him. He might do something foolish or dangerous," Tommy said.

Chapter 28
The Black Chest

The next morning Grella went straight to the Earth room. She found Counselor Golden polishing a dinosaur bone. He had a fluffy white beard and looked like a friendly grandpa. He also reminded Grella of a squashed pumpkin, short and wide. His oozing belly spilled over his belt. .

"I heard worms were one of your special subjects. May I ask you some questions about them?"

"What would we do without worms! They're amazing creations. Of course I'd be delighted to answer your questions. What did you say your name was?"

"Grella Weller," Grella said

Counselor Golden never looked up, but he listened to Grella's questions about worms.

She spent the next twenty minutes watching the Counselor polish bones while he talked to her about wormology, the study of worms. He recommended several books for her to read.

"You're sure you have the titles right? Read the list back to me." Counselor Golden was noted for being thorough.

Grella looked down at her notepad: "*Worm Lover's World, Edy the Earthworm, and Worms —Silent Heroes of Earth.*"

"That's right. You're in for exciting reading."

"Counselor Golden, you've been very helpful. I'll definitely check out these books with Filey. Before I go, Counselor, I've heard about your famous Black Nature Chest. May I look inside it? That's it over in the corner, isn't it?" She pointed at a chest about three feet high that sat on short carved legs.

"Artifact Chest, my dear girl. That's the correct term. If you've heard about the Chest, you must know it's only for campers currently in this session."

Grella's eyelids fluttered. "I'm disappointed —such fascinating items for study."

"Yes, I've treasures in there, no doubt about it. Although treasure is always in the eye of the looker. Not everyone sees what I do."

"Counselor Golden, I bet the campers love this activity." It sounded to Grella like she was buttering him up, but she was being truthful.

"Not every camper, it's sad." Counselor Golden looked up. "Some campers have absolutely no curiosity. I can't imagine where they lost it." Then his face brightened a bit. "But, for some, that's why they've been sent to Dunster's. My job is to help them rediscover enthusiasm and curiosity."

"How awful not to be curious."

"Oh imagination doesn't disappear entirely," Counselor Golden said, "it just gets buried deep down and needs triggers to get it back. I can almost always stir imagination up again in campers when I work with them."

"Like getting campers excited about the Artifact Chest?"

"Exactly!" he shouted. "That's one way. A peek in there can do amazing things."

Grella's eyes blazed with longing. After the incident in Director Croggle's office she knew better than to look without permission. "Counselor Golden, I know you said no, but I must ask again. It's very important to me. May I please take a quick look?"

"Well." He began rubbing the bone in his hand with more vigor.

"I can't take your Wonder sessions for two weeks. And the items in the chest will probably all be changed by then," Grella coaxed.

"Hmmm." Counselor Golden lifted his eyes toward the ceiling light. He rubbed his little mustache and seemed to be considering carefully. "Quite likely these items will be changed soon. There's a new wonder coming in all the time. Once I get campers hunting for them, they can't seem to stop. Why I almost need a bigger chest again! It's already three times bigger than the one I had during my first year as a counselor."

Grella sensed he was close to a yes. "It would be so interesting to see!" Grella clenched her teeth.

Splack! His decision hit the air between them. He'd decided. She knew it. She saw it in his eyes before he said it.

"Well, I know you're a wonder-er already with your worm research and all. I suppose I could let you take a peek. Don't tell the other campers though."

Counselor Golden walked across the room to the chest. He removed a key chain from his pocket, unlocked the large black chest and raised the lid.

Grella followed behind him. When she looked inside she saw vibrant-colored leaves and twigs of various shapes, labeled vials of water and rocks that looked like crystals. Then she saw the stone! A large golden stone! It was the same kind as their earlier clue only five times bigger. She lifted it up and felt the bottom. Taped underneath were envelopes.

She saw Counselor Golden watching her closely. Then he did something quite unusual. He winked at her, and said, "Take anything you please."

"I can?"

He turned and walked over to his raccoon cages. "You'll be freed tonight, my raccoon friends, now don't you worry." At first Grella thought he was talking to her, but then realized he was speaking to the animals.

When Counselor Golden came back over Grella had closed the chest and replaced the stone minus one envelope.

Counselor Golden winked at her a second time and said, "Perseverance, sticking-to-it as long as it takes, that's what every thinker and dreamer needs. I see you've already got that Grella Weller. No need to take my Wonder sessions in two weeks, but I hope you'll come. You'll do well."

"Oh, thank you." Grella smiled graciously and hurried out.

Outside the door of Golden's room, Grella tore open the envelope and read the next clue:

"Golden stones, silver swords,

Power and might,

You need them all for the test tonight,

The Trail of Terror is no delight.

Find your way with no delay.

Only one may go.

Beware if you stray."

Her fingers shook as she replaced the note. She had to get this clue to her Silver Team immediately. Who would be willing go on the Trail of Terror after reading this? Not her! She shivered and took off on a run.

Grella flew through the halls and was nearly to the dorm wing when something unthinkable and horrible happened.

She ran smack into Counselor Pettypoint, Master Monitor of Dunster's Halls and Dorms.

Pettypoint's name fit her well. She had a pointy chin, pointy fingers, even a bit of a pointy noise. She was tall enough to have been a good match for Counselor Spindlesticks although no one had ever actually seen them talking to one another.

Pettypoint wore a black hairnet that kept her braided bun in place. It reminded Grella of a spider's lair. The counselor stood at points of the hall where she couldn't be easily seen, until you rounded the corner. Then she pounced upon her prey, her eyes scouring campers for the least hint of unsuitable behavior.

Few Dunnies had escaped her discipline. Until this moment Grella had been lucky. Especially since Grella liked running better than walking, even when she wasn't hurrying toward the dorm carrying valuable information.

Counselor Pettypoint's reputation was whispered about from day one of camp. When she pounced there was no quick or easy getaway.

"Young lady," the Counselor said firmly and almost loud enough to be heard in the next building, "have you EVER heard the rule, 'No running in the hall'? We have acres of grounds to run on outside. In this building there are great minds at work on inventions and we can't have disturbance in the halls."

"I'm sorry Counselor, I thought I was only walking fast. I must have sped up a bit without thinking. Very kind of you to remind me. I'll slow down now."

"Now!" Pettypoint screeched out the word. "Now that you've been caught, you'll slow down!" She drew back as if Grella had thrust a knife into her neck. "Well it doesn't work that easily!"

Grella's legs trembled.

Counselor Pettypoint continued. "A rule is a rule is a rule!"

Grella's fingers holding the envelope shook. She almost dropped it on Pettypoint's pointed boots.

"And what is that envelope in your hand? Sending mail by old-fashioned letters! Don't you know this is a special camp? We've a reputation to live up to! E-mail or D-mail or no mail!" D-mail, Grella had been told, was the wall tube system invented by a camper of Dunster's, a graduate of the tenth camp held.

Grella stared at the envelope in her hand. Why hadn't she hidden it?

"It's nothing," Grella said. "It's not correspondence really."

Evidently Pettypoint didn't know that Mystery Card clues came in envelopes. She paid no attention to the campers' mystery work. Why would she? She cared about only one thing —rules.

"It certainly looks like something," she barked.

"I mean nothing of importance to you, Counselor Pettypoint."

"I'll decide that! Give it to me."

At that moment Piney came running around the corner followed by Migtwee, the cat.

Pettypoint's cheeks turned magenta.

"Another runner! Stop!"

Piney ran past Pettypoint with Migtwee on his heels.

Counselor Pettypoint pulled her whistle from her wrist bracelet and blew. Grella covered her ears at the shrill sound.

"Stop, I said! Stop!"

Piney froze into a block of human ice. "Sorry, mam."

"Another sorry! A rule is a rule is a rule. Come over here!"

Piney came nearer sheepishly, stopping about six feet away.

"Do you think this is a racetrack?"

"No, mam."

"Not mam, Counselor Pettypoint to you. Come closer so I can see you better." Pettypoint was already striding toward him.

"Yes, mam, I mean Counselor," Piney said.

Pettypoint started to scribble out an activity penalty on her notepad using the pencil hanging around her neck. She always kept it tied there, ready for a fast draw.

"See how you enjoy this, Mr. Putilla. You're dismissed from camp activities the rest of today and confined to your room."

"Not all day!" Piney pleaded.

"Yes, all day and be sure to close the door. You may not have visitors! No stimulation is allowed OF ANY KIND!"

Tommy heard the commotion in the hall and peeked out of his room as Pettypoint was lecturing Piney.

Grella saw him, and frantically waved the envelope in her hand at him.

Somehow she made Tommy understand her peril. He ducked back in his room and pulled an old envelope from his drawer. Then he scratched out some words on a paper, stuck it inside and sealed it.

Tommy sauntered casually out of his room toward the group. Pettypoint was making such a point of disciplining Piney that she didn't even notice Tommy approach.

When Tommy reached Grella he hastily switched envelopes with her as he passed. He quickly shoved Grella's envelope into the pocket of his pants —the navy blue ones Dunnies wore on Mondays and Wednesdays easily concealed the envelope.

He'd come not a second too soon. Counselor Pettypoint dismissed Piney. Then she hiked back toward the waiting Grella.

Tommy continued walking down the hall. His movement was only a little faster than a slow snail.

Grella braced herself.

Outside the hall window the last stalks of sunlight swept the sky clearing away another day. Grella wished she were outside enjoying the evening.

"Now young lady, that envelope!"

Pettypoint snatched it from Grella's hand, ripped it open and began to read, "'Who Wants To Be A Dunster's Billionaire? Your next question is: What is the national bird of the United States, the sparrow, Big Bird, or the parakeet?'"

"This is the silliest waste of paper I've ever seen! Everyone knows none of these answers is correct."

"It's, err... for a game."

Counselor Pettypoint tossed the envelope back at Grella with a look of disgust. "I hope you and your team can use your brains better than this. No wonder your mystery isn't solved yet!"

"Yes, Counselor Pettypoint."

"Now off with you, and don't ever let me ever catch you sending correspondence the old-fashioned way again!" She click-clacked down the hall in her pointy brown high heels.

Grella took a deep breath. At least the envelope had distracted Pettypoint from Grella's running. Thank you Sunmaker. Some human rules are breakable in emergencies; help me to always know the difference.

Back in his room Tommy opened the envelope and read the clue. He shuddered at the words, "Trail of Terror."

Who would go?

Chapter 29
Trail of Terror

As leader of the Silver Team Tommy decided he should be the one to go on the Trail of Terror. He wasn't feeling good about it.

The horror stories of those who had started upon it were whispered after midnight in darkened dorm rooms. The Trail was the one place no Dunnie wanted to go.

Tommy made his plans privately and told no one. His team might want to shadow him to provide protection. The instructions were to go alone.

The trail started at the edge of the North woods. The beginning was marked by a simple "T."

Tommy squared his shoulders and started out on the bramble and bug-infested path shortly after dark. Locusts buzzed him like dive-bombers. They attacked his face viciously and crawled in his hair. Thorns the size of icicles scraped his skin. Several drew blood.

Something even more insidious was happening within him. He began to get impatient, mildly at first, then furious. Why was he the one to go on this? Why couldn't he ever get the help he needed! What was it about this place anyway? Why had he even come to Dunster's Camp?

Rage spread over his body like a huge blanket smothering his kindness and tolerance. It stripped away every trace of happiness. Tommy struggled against these angry feelings but his self-control was slipping away also. Fury settled upon him.

Hadn't he worked harder than anyone to solve the mystery? Why should his friends get any credit?

Who did those counselors think they were with all their demands anyway? Tommy began to drown in hate. He tried with all his mental strength to pull himself out.

Was this a Drubbin after him? He looked around, but saw no one. *It must be Dagta,* Tommy thought. *He's trying to destroy me.*

"Sunmaker, please help," Tommy said aloud. Evil and hate waged a war against goodness and love inside Tommy. His mouth wanted to shout ugly words. His brain broiled with mean thoughts.

His heart beat faster, his blood raced like the track of a speed car race. Sunmaker, I just want to hate. Let me hate. Help! I can't stop this alone.

"No! Stop!" The Sunmaker spoke to Tommy's heart, "Think of doing good to yourself and others. Be ready to forgive those who hurt you."

Little by little, not instantly, Tommy began to be filled with tenderness toward his teammates again and even for the negative and mean campers. Anger still surged, but his rage began to soften.

Tommy prayed aloud. "I want to be in control of my thoughts, Sunmaker. Help me."

The demon of Rage brought fresh fire. Tommy smelled a trail of smoke as he walked. He fell, got up and stomped forward again.

A rock blocked his path. Tommy was tempted to slam his body into it. "Nothing and nobody better get in my way." Hate was sweet at first. He liked the taste of it in his mouth.

He forced himself to take another way around.

A voice inside his head said, "Stop, these thoughts are wrong."

"I don't want to stop. I want to hate," Tommy said aloud.

"No, you don't," came the quiet voice deep within him.

In Tommy's imagination, someone who looked like Grella ran after him.

She caught up with him and said, "Tommy, what's wrong with you?" He couldn't look at her.

His smile was a snarl. His eyes black stones. "Get away from me," he screamed. He covered his ears when she spoke.

"Come back, Tommy," she begged, "don't give in to Dagta attacking your emotions. This isn't you."

His head pounded. Stop knocking on my head, Dagta. Even in his wildness he knew Dagta was part of this, but he didn't care.

"Take control and choose hope." Grella's voice screamed in his mind.

"I can't."

"You can —you must!"

Tommy tried to reach the feeling in her words. It was too hard to climb over the mounds of rage in his way. Somewhere deep within he knew the image of Grella was right. Why was he thinking of her? She wasn't here. Was she praying for him right now?

Tommy clenched his fists. His nails dug into his skin.

He heard words spoken with boldness. "Leave him, Dagta. He's mine."

The next moment Tommy found himself lying flat on the ground totally exhausted.

"Sunmaker, I'm free."

"Yes, but Dagta will try again. Use your protection."

Tommy remembered the Holy Words he'd learned.

When Dagta returned, Tommy was ready. He flung words of truth at him: "Revenge is the Sunmaker's, not mine.

He will punish wrongs. I am to finish the work I've been given. I can do all things through Him who gives me strength."

Suddenly a huge mass stood before Tommy's eyes. This had to be Dagta. Tommy staggered up almost unable to believe what he was seeing. The mammoth shape started shrinking.

In seconds Dagta was transformed from to a wisp of smoke. Finally there was a poof and he disappeared altogether. Only his voice boomed out, "I'll be back."

"And I'll be ready!" Tommy yelled in the direction of the sound. "I'm going to stay on the Trail of Terror as long as it takes. You can't stop me!"

Tommy reminded himself he was the Silver Team leader. He would not let his team down. He could face any danger on this forsaken Trail of Terror.

The trail wound through more bramble bush. Trees were covered with thick vines ready to crawl around Tommy's neck and choke him if he got too close.

At the next bend Tommy stumbled upon a burlap bag the size of a ten-pound sack of potatoes. It had a silver star on it. Could that mean it was for the Silver Team?

Tommy leaned against a huge oak and opened the drawstring. It was too dark to examine the contents clearly, but inside he felt boxes. He took them out one by one and counted in amazement up to seven – one for each team member. He put them away just in time.

Standing in the darkness ahead was a dreaded cloaked shape towering as high as a roof. Dagta was illuminated by an icy whiteness —the coldest white Tommy had ever seen.

The figure held out two hands in an embrace. Tommy shuddered at the glistening, frost-like, pitted metal fingers that looked like they could squeeze life from bones.

The sight was visible for only a split second and then gone. Or was it? Tommy blinked and blinked again.

He sensed, rather than saw, the iciness coming at him from behind. He turned to see Dagta again in full livid ugliness. Black lines streaked his face. Thick white fingers reached out to snatch the bag Tommy held.

Tommy clutched it tighter. He wanted to run, but couldn't move. His feet had planted themselves like oak tree roots. Tommy felt an intense heat sweeping over him. Dagta's breath burned like a fire in his chest. The fire pierced deep into his very heart.

Tommy struggled to stay on his feet. He croaked, "Get out of my way."

Tommy heard Dagta laugh, but saw only black pointed teeth moving. The next sound was the licking of flames. Tommy felt himself being dragged toward a terrible deep coldness even as the crackling of the fire grew louder. He tried to speak again, but couldn't. A thick heat was swirling inside him. Someone was calling him back.

All around him people screamed for help. He couldn't help them. He couldn't even help himself.

Tommy tried to make his arms and legs move but they were like lead pipes.

Then everything went black and he passed out.

He didn't know how long he was out, but when Tommy awoke he was lying in the grass at the edge of the North woods. He felt like he was in a walk-in freezer. Blankets were being piled on him by Grella.

His eyelids fluttered.

Piney rushed up. "Are you okay?"

Tommy couldn't talk. His teeth wouldn't stop shaking.

"Oh Tommy, tell us you're alright. We found you in a terrible state. What a fright we've had."

Tommy's body felt like the day he came down with the chicken pox. "How are the others?" He finally managed to ask.

"Who?" Grella and Piney looked at each other bewildered. They thought he'd been alone.

"The people begging for help out on the Trail of Terror with me. I tried to help them —I couldn't."

"Rest now," Grella said flashing Piney a look of alarm.

"But I saw Dagta," Tommy said weakly.

He had seen him, hadn't he? He never could have made up a sight like that. Tommy started to shiver as the image returned fresh in his mind. He'd been so fearful, but he survived. How?

The Sunmaker answered. "*Only my power can fight Dagta. You know truth. You will always survive. With knowledge of Me comes My help.*"

"Ohhhh," Tommy moaned aloud.

Blake handed him a raspberry yogurt and a plastic spoon from his pant's pocket. "Eat this. You'll feel better."

"Later, thanks." Tommy pushed the food away and half sat up. "The mystery! The bag! Where is it?" His hands groped agitatedly on the ground on both sides of him until he touched the burlap bag. "What time is it?"

When they told him he said, "You mean I was only in there a little over an hour. It seemed like half of forever."

He struggled to his feet. "I must show you —help me, Piney," Tommy ordered. "I need to lean on you until my legs feel stronger. I want to give you something."

The wide-eyed team members gathered around Tommy. Not only had he survived the Trail of Terror, but he'd found something!

He reached for the bag and opened it for all to see.

Chapter 30
The Boxes of Three

"These must be a clue," Grella said, "But it's so strange, all these boxes. What do you make of it?"

"I don't know," Tommy said. "We've always had envelopes before, except for the one box from the Sunmaker, but never individual boxes for everyone. Go get the rest of the team. We'll open them together."

Grella hurried back to the camp. She was about to break into a run when she saw Counselor Pettypoint turning the corner. Grella stopped and proceeded at a tortoise pace.

Twenty minutes later she was back with the missing team members.

Tommy passed around the boxes.

Each box tied with a shimmering silver ribbon had a personal nametag. Tommy's tag read, "Tommy Smurlee, Team Leader."

Tommy's box also had a small red envelope taped to the top. Inside he found a Mystery Clue Card. He read aloud, "These objects are for each of you. But you must know what they represent before you can use them to solve the mystery."

Blake interrupted, "Let's open them!"

Grella yelled, "Wait! Shouldn't Tommy finish reading the card first?"

Blake's hand was already tugging on the bow. "C'mon, everybody at the same time. Let's see what we got. Ready?"

"Whoah," Tommy ordered. "I need to at least read the rest of this to myself and see if it's okay to go on." He dropped his eyes back to the letter he held.

The Silver Team waited. No one moved.

"Is it alright to open them?" Blake asked again.

Tommy looked up. "Okay, open them."

A noisy shuffling of paper and cardboard followed.

Toodle pulled out a rock.

"I have one too," Quid said, "and a mirror the size of a small pancake."

"I have the same things and there's something else. A key!" Grella said.

Tommy asked, "Does everybody have three items?"

"Yes."

"Okay," Tommy continued, "here's the rest of the letter. The rock is to remind you that the Sunmaker is always solid and strong and dependable. Rocks don't disappear, neither will He. He always will be there for you."

Maryna shut her eyes tight. She intended to remember.

"The mirror is to see yourself —a creation of the Sunmaker, for you are made in His image. Keep all these items as reminders of what they represent."

Tommy continued to read. "The key is a reminder to unlock your unique abilities and use them for yourself and for others, too."

Toodle clutched his key tightly.

"Also each key will open the door to the Dreamology Lab where you'll find your next clue."

"On the main computer open to the file named Mystery. It will only open between the hours of midnight and 12:15 a.m. Make sure no member from another team enters with you. If they go online at the same time, they can destroy the final Mystery Clue."

At 12:03 they were all in the lab with the overhead lights beaming down.

"I saw Orson's cat, Migtwee, hiding in a corner as we were coming down the hallway," Grella said.

"Usually he's with Orson," Quid said. "I wonder if we're being followed."

"Lock the door," Maryna said.

Mr. Toodle's knees started to shake.

"We'll get in and out before Orson comes," Quid said. "Quick, let's barricade the door just in case. Help me move the chairs against it."

Blake logged on. "Shut off the overhead lights, we have enough light coming from the computer screen."

Blake opened to the Mystery File.

Grella read from the screen as Tommy scrolled down: "Three questions are all that remain between you and victory. You've been through the tunnel and the hedge, you've survived the Trail of Terror and used your reasoning powers, now we'll check your overall knowledge. Listen to the questions carefully and type in your answer."

"Question One is about history." The screen flashed three times to a paragraph of text.

Grella read, "Who failed often but never gave up? He went on to become one of America's greatest Presidents. One of his famous quotes is, 'Stand with anybody who stands right, but part with him, when he goes wrong.'"

Tommy said, "I think it's Abraham Lincoln. He had many failures in his life before he became President." The computer keys clicked as Tommy entered the name.

Three beeps sounded and the screen flashed in large neon green letters, CORRECT.

"Read the next one, Grella," Piney said.

They heard a loud thump and the sound of voices out in the hall.

"Shhh!" Toodle whispered. Piney quietly pressed his weight against the chairs blocking the door. They waited until the steps faded away. The next question is a riddle," Grella read, "I'm everywhere and you need me. You can't touch me or see me. I'm very valuable, yet I'm free. Figure out this riddle and you may go to Question number three."

"Maybe the answer is time?" Piney said.

The computer buzzed and the computer screen flashed red.

"Wrong, it must be something else. We have seven minutes left," Tommy said.

Blake pounded his fist against his head. "I can't imagine what."

"Yes, you can," Quid said. He sat down, chin in his hand. He didn't say anything for several seconds. Then he jumped to his feet.

"Air! " Quid said. "It's the air we breathe."

"That could be it." Tommy punched in the word.

They watched the screen turn green.

"Right!" Tommy yelled.

Piney cleared his throat. "Listen," he said, "the footsteps are coming back."

"The last question, number three, is, Identify the person on Dunster's staff who created this year's Great Unsolved Mystery. Remember you only get seven guesses. Here are your clues."

Tommy read, "Heights he likes, authors he cites, you've won the game if you get him right. Time is tight, you've one more minute starting now." A clock face appeared on the computer set to sixty seconds."

Piney said, "It had to be Zeller, you know how strange he was acting.

"No, he's too obvious," Tommy said.

Quid said, "What about Tinns on the fifth floor?"

"He could have been there to throw us off. But, okay try him," Tommy ordered.

Red flashed. Wrong answer came on the screen. Six more chances.

Toodle shouted out another counselor's name, "Wishkowski. Dreams can take you anywhere. Try him."

Another wrong answer.

"Try Hintley. He likes to climb mountains and he talks about books and authors," Grella shouted.

The screen turned red.

"Zolten is always reading," Maryna offered.

"But he has nothing to do with heights."

Tommy checked the time. Only thirty seconds left. "Team, we've got to hurry, I know we can do this."

"Counselor Kutilda is a trapeze artist, that's high," Piney shouted at the computer.

Still no green and they were down to their last guess.

"Maybe the staff person is not a counselor," Tommy said.

"You mean Director Croggle? No way," Quid said.

"No, I'm thinking of someone else. Maybe it's," Tommy's eyes brightened, "Filey!"

"Filey?" Piney repeated.

"Yes, the little man who gives us our equipment when camp starts, the Keeper of the Supplies. You know how he loves his books and he's on the attic floor. That's as high as you can go," Tommy said.

"Try him," everyone agreed.

The screen flashed green.

"Congratulations. You have solved the mystery. Now your entire team must report the answers to these questions to Director Croggle. He is being notified that someone has mastered the mystery. He will meet you in his office."

Everybody whooped and hollered as they took the chairs away from the door and opened it. Suddenly they stopped in silence.

Orson was outside listening. Three of his team members were with him.

Orson stormed into the room, rushed past Tommy and turned the computer on. Meanwhile Orson's team members tried to grab Tommy. Quid put his head down like a ramming bull and ran headlong into the stomach of the first boy in the way. As the boy fell he knocked the other two down. Tommy and the team had just enough time to get through the door before they recovered.

Tommy and the Silver Team hurried down the hall.

"This is bad. Orson may have heard our last answer. We were too loud. It won't take long for him to go through the other two questions," Piney said puffing for breath.

How much time did they have before Orson's team followed? Tommy wondered. "Orson won't win if we report the answers to Director Croggle first!"

The Silver Team members piled one at a time onto the Wind Whoosher.

They were panting breathlessly by the time they reached the main office. Croggle wasn't in his office, only Viola, his secretary.

"Where is Director Croggle? We must see him!"

"Do you know what time it is? He doesn't like being awakened in the middle of the night. I'm only here because he asked me to do some extra work tonight."

Tommy insisted that Viola page the Director. "This is an emergency, he's supposed to be here. "

She quickly looked Tommy over and the crew with him. "About what? If you're sick or injured, I'll call the camp nurse."

Tommy stiffened and spoke firmly. "We must speak with the Director."

Viola harrumphed. She liked to know everything that was going on.

Apparently this didn't look like an emergency to her. She took her time with the page.

"What if Orson meets him in the hall before he gets in here?" Maryna asked.

"We'll have to take that chance," Grella said.

"Here comes Croggle."

They all shouted at once. "We solved the mystery." Quickly they recited the answers to the questions, "Abraham Lincoln, air and Filey."

Croggle smiled. "We thought using Filey was a stroke of genius."

Just then Orson came running in with his team members close behind. "I've solved it," he said, rattling off the answers.

"Sorry, Orson, you're too late. Maybe next year."

***

The last day of camp the Dunnies were together in the Great Hall when Croggle made the announcement. "Silver Team, I declare you the Winner of This Year's Dunster's Great Unsolved Mystery. I thought sure this year the staff had our campers stumped."

"Not us, sir," Mr. Toodle said.

Proudly each Silver Team member came forward and received a trophy with the year engraved under "Dunster's Camp of Mystery and Inventions" and a huge gold medal engraved with "I Solved Dunster's Great Unsolved Mystery." Other ribbons were also awarded.

Tommy looked around. He knew he'd never forget this summer. Cheers went up from the other campers. "Yeah, Silver Team. Yeah!"

Tommy smiled and nudged Toodle, "I knew we could do it."

Toodle grinned as he rubbed his medal.

Counselor Wudderbuster waddled to the speaker's platform. "Next year you're invited to return to Dunster's if you dare. Our mystery teams will have the challenge of finding the missing life-size statue of our camp founder, Conrad Dunster. Camp Dunster's will officially close until next June, except for the offices of our permanent staff who will continue with their on-going research and inventions."

The campers filed out sadly, wishing they could start the new search immediately.

"It's a good thing camp is ending. I need a rest," Molar Malone said at their final team meeting in Tommy and Piney's room. "I've been working way too hard on this mystery."

The rest of the Silver Team looked at their back-up team member who had done nothing and chuckled. No one said anything.

"I heard Orson left for home already. Is that true?" Tommy asked.

"Yes. He stormed off in a fit right after Counselor Wudderbuster announced us as the winners," Blake said.

"I hope he doesn't come back next year," Maryna said.

"He will, and he'll be as mean as ever," Quid added.

"Well I'm not even going to think about him until then," Grella said.

"That's the spirit." Blake said. "Bye, guys, I'm going to be the first to leave."

"Yes, Blake, why don't you go first for a change," Piney said.

They all laughed, and went their separate ways, promising to return next year.

Read The Next Book in Adventures of Tommy Smurlee
Series:

Tommy Smurlee and the Missing Statue

About the Author

Judith Rolfs writes fiction and non-fiction for all ages.
She creates pictures with words that bring laughter, suspense
and
challenge to the minds and hearts of children.
She's a lover of truth and a respecter of the power of words.
A self-appointed guardian of imagination,
Judith Rolfs is committed
to the development of positive values and creativity.

**For other books by Judith Rolfs
check your local or on-line bookstore.**

**Visit her website at www.judithrolfs.com
Become a friend of Tommy Smurlee on Facebook.**

Made in the USA
Middletown, DE
07 May 2019